the concerto inn

University of Western Australia Press New Writing Series

In 2005, its seventieth year of publishing outstanding academic and general titles, UWA Press launched a New Writing series, with a focus on creative writing. We are sourcing novels and shorter prose works from postgraduate creative writing programs in universities across Australia, which for the last three decades have produced exciting new works from emerging and established writers. By introducing this series, we are recognising the role of Australian universities in nurturing and supporting writers, and contributing to the continuing production of Australian writing.

Series editor Terri-ann White is actively involved in the literary culture of Australia: as a writer, bookseller, editor and award judge. Her novel *Finding Theodore and Brina* (2001) is studied in university courses in Spain, the United States and Australia. She published a collection of stories, *Night and Day*, in 1994, has edited anthologies and been published widely. She is currently director of both UWA Press and a cross-disciplinary research centre at The University of Western Australia.

Titles in series

A New Map of the Universe, Annabel Smith
Cusp, Josephine Wilson
The Concerto Inn, Jo Gardiner

the
CONCERTO
INN

Jo Gardiner

University of Western Australia Press

University of Western Australia Press
Crawley, Western Australia 6009
www.uwapress.uwa.edu.au

National Library of Australia
Cataloguing-in-Publication entry:

Gardiner, Jo.
The Concerto Inn.
ISBN 1 920694 79 X.
ISBN 978 1 920694 79 1
I. Title
A823.4

Cover photograph by Gary Isaacs
www.garyisaacs.com   *Consultant editor Amanda Curtin
Designed by Robyn Mundy
Typeset in 10 pt Janson by Lasertype
Printed by McPherson's Printing Group*

Brian, this book is for you

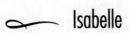 Isabelle

There is a long phrase between the night notes, the end notes by the bell, then this brimming morning reverie in windflowers, Italian lavender, sea anemones and *Bellis perennis*. Slaked lime and marble dust make polished plaster of the air; the budding gardenia rests a heavy head; dogwood leaves lie against the sky like boats on still water. In the weeping mulberry a swaying worm spits silk. An azalea flower drops to the earth, like a bright pink origami bird.

In this generous dwelling, a breath away from summer, she stands in the mosaic of the moment, listening for the next note of the struck bell, beneath the desiccating blossom of the pear tree; the sun first upon her head, then shoulders, in sheets of smoking gold. She stands tall and quite still, an iris gloved in green. Around her, forget-me-nots are rocked by bees and she can hear the panting of birds' wings. The scent of bergamot orange is like a veil across her face.

In a pool of night rain, the water swells with light under its skin, reflecting pale iris with yellow throats, stroke after stroke of ixia stacked on pearwood, the luminous muslin spider web, spent flowers like empty cicada shells.

⌐

The glissandi of currawong voices echo like running water in the morning.

In this illuminated manuscript of broken colour, the blue glaze of her eye is set upon the Rottweiler at the end of the road...

Falling, falling

Hong Kong.

The words form like two bubbles of blood. Hong Kong: the collision of two texts. Betrayed by Britain, reauthored by China.

Here, the rain comes straight down. Plum rain.

Goodbye, Philippe, I whisper very early each morning, leaving you sleeping as I walk from the university up the dark rock mountain to the Peak, above the pea-green harbour. I don't know what I'm training for. The concrete path winds through bauhinia trees. It is late September 1994, unseasonally hot and humid, and the odour of autumn decay is everywhere, brown leaves curling in the heavy darkness of the undergrowth along the path that leads up to Hatton Road. Halfway, I stop at a hut and turn back to see the harbour below, still now, beneath the heavy air.

I hear a sound like tap dancing before rounding the corner and meeting the man who smacks his forehead with one hand while he walks. We pass each other on the narrow cement path.

Jo sun, Isabelle.

Jo sun.

Elderly men and women, who walk in the groups of the villages they have left behind in China, greet me and become my silent companions.

Each day, after I return from my walk, we share a breakfast of fruit and tea in the dining room. And then you descend to write in your office in the old building, and I set off to find the travelator and ride to Central. Today I get off halfway down and wander the streets with my camera until I come across a street lined with cane baskets full of dried coin snakes and seahorses. I lean over to photograph the dark shapes repeating themselves under hot lights.

On Ice House Street I find an antique map, and upon my return place it on the desk at the residence that will be my home for a time. I unfurl it, pass my hand across the wash of colour, hear the scrape of silk, allow it to spring back into a scroll. As you sit further down the mountain in your office, I hear my voice tell you of the treasure I have found for you, for your novel, Philippe, a map of the Silk Road where travellers met wild beasts in steaming valleys and journeyed from the stone tower to a place called *This*. Caravanserais of the gods. The celestial horses of Kokand, sweating blood, watched traders carry Seric cloth to the gynaeceums of Constantinople, to produce sumptuous brocades from tiny birds' feathers. Opus plumarium. And flower tissue.

And not simply silk. Stones that shone in the night, phosphorescent with the bile of the tortoise. Red coral, yellow amber, marble, cinnabar, green jade, the samite used for ecclesiastic vestments, sendal, brocade from Andalusia, baldachins embossed with gold…

The words fall from me like the soft wings of blue silk thrown over the shoulders of women from Damascus. It is the enchantment of distance I feel.

Outside, the asphalt burns. My tongue settles on the floor of my mouth and I become silent, simply a receiver of sound, light and colour. My eyes move slowly in my face, stopped by the thick air from seeing the sun; I do not know east from west unless I look towards Guangzhou to the north, where the planes settle at Kai Tak. Read the city according to the harbour.

In this northern hemisphere my blood moves in different directions.

❧

You left Katoomba before me and travelled to Guangzhou and the conference. I remained to finalise the classes I had been teaching at the local high school, but my mind was set upon the journey I would make.

You rang me from China. Your paper had been well received. Dr Rose, the lecturer in Romance languages, had been located, and you had teamed up. She was arranging our accommodation at the university. Soon we would be reunited in Hong Kong. Just a few more weeks. One evening I rang the White Swan Hotel. A woman answered. She spoke softly and I thought that it must have been very late in China. There was no answer in your room.

❧

As the plane moved between the buildings, I saw a family eating dinner, their chopsticks working like scissors above their bowls. I walked into the terminal at Kai Tak, the humidity enfolding me and brightening the lights of Kowloon.

You were standing behind the barrier, your hands in your pockets. At first you did not see me. When I kissed you, there was a strange new scent. I laughed and asked what it was. Drakkar Noir, you said, dragging out the soft *oir* sound. Here was a new energy in you, an inclination to laugh, something that had been absent for so long.

The car took us under the harbour, up the mountain from Central to the university, and as we passed through the darkness you told me about the group from the university who went out together for the moon festival on the night of the lanterns. You ate mooncakes for the first time since you were a child growing up in Hong Kong with your French mother and Australian father. You had gone to visit the place where you lived in Pokfulam. The ledge where you used to hide your toy cars on your way to school was still there. You even ran your finger along it.

Setting the scene for me, you told me that the university was on the western side of Hong Kong Island. Painted red with a dark tiled roof, the residence sat at the top of the campus to accommodate international visitors. Verandahs ran around each floor, and the blocks were linked by a series of courtyards. Large, shiny black doors led out onto Conduit Road.

You told me that the path down to the rest of the university passed through the Run Run Shaw Building and the K. K. Leung Building to the library, which was a sweep of concrete. Your office was in the old building below that, built of red brick with cream edges and arches, glass, some wood. It looked out onto a courtyard, where there were palm trees and a round fish pond in the centre. A belltower overlooked the courtyard.

Arriving at the residence, we carried the luggage to flat forty-one, which had a sitting area, a bedroom and a bathroom with a tiny transparent lizard on the tiles. Beside the television, on the desk, was a present for me from Guangzhou, a box covered in ornate green cloth, with a label of Chinese characters. It had white latches and, inside, five Chinese pens tied to the roof of the box. Their stems were made from wood of varying thickness. On the floor of the box was a pot of black ink.

I laughed. Pleased with the gift, the reunion, with the time ahead in Hong Kong.

～

The Fung Ping Shan Museum at the university, opposite the school on Bonham Strand, is a perfect disc enclosing smaller ones, and we climb its ever-decreasing circles to see Escher's early lithographs, his depictions of the Amalfi Coast, and the complexity of its gaze out to sea. When you move away, anxious to get back to the office to write, I remain a while longer in front of the pure lines that enter my open heart, and hear myself say aloud: I will go to Ravello.

～

We will go to Macau today, leaving the rock and its shadow for the day.

In Queens Road Central a woman's face is white in a way that reminds me of a winding sheet. She is tall with black hair drawn back from her neck. I see that she has been very ill. A white mask covers her mouth. Taking very small steps, she walks tentatively with her eyes downcast, supported at the elbow by another woman. I avoid her carefully on the street and wait for you at the Macau ferry pier in Sheung Wan, the heat wet on my neck. When you arrive at the last minute, you are out of breath.

Crossing the Pearl River estuary to Macau, there is the sullenness of the water and sky. Along its edges, the land is being reclaimed against its will.

A taxi takes us to the Avenida da Republica, where we find the Pousada de Sao Tiago and the film director. Underneath his black jacket is a black T-shirt with a red rectangle across the chest. The brim of his hat is curled back where his hands have often felt for it. We sit in his room and you discuss the progress of the screenplay and film locations. Then the three of us take a taxi. The driver stumbles over the directions as we drive along the waterfront. Foxing. He draws out his street directory with a heavy shrug of his shoulders. The film director is enraged.

There, he stabs at the driver, pointing up to the yellow and white Bela Vista Hotel, directly above us on the side of the Colina da Penha. There is a heavy silence as the taxi winds its way up to the hotel. As he thrusts money at the driver, the film director turns to you.

We might be able to use this place as I suggested, Philippe, he says. See what you think.

On the verandah of the hotel the film director takes off his hat. The light gives soft fur to his bald head as he turns towards us in his chair and leans his elbow on the table. He lights a cigarette and then holds it in thick, square fingers as if it is a flute that he raises to his lips to play from time to time. The broad fall of his forehead is underlined by heavy brows above steady eyes, a large nose, mouth. He frowns, remembering the taxi driver.

Fool.

Collects himself.

Now, lunch.

There is a lemon, wrapped in muslin, to be squeezed over the caesar salad. And jazz. The dazed eyes of the young saxophonist look surprised to find his best breath is into the instrument. He plays 'Cow-Cow Boogie'.

Your eyes are averted. In the mirror above the bar, I see them. They come from a place where there is a river, where several streams become one. There in the depths of the hills, transparent, smooth green stones are washed down by the heavy rain. They are scooped out of the water from a small boat. They are said to be the reflection of stars shining on the earth's surface and hardened there.

You contemplate the fall of Macau to the Praia Grande Bay, Taipa across the bridge in the yellow light, the decay. You don't speak. There is a quarry, an open-cut mine in meaning, that the film director ignores as he describes his film about memory happening back in Australia now, and the phone calls to and fro in the middle of the night. He tells me of his problem with Proust, how he could never get past those biscuits. I smile and think of my father reading aloud to Madeleine and me by the fire.

You are looking at the famous bar room with the bullet hole in the mirror. Perhaps you dream of your childhood when you holidayed with your mother in the Bela Vista, while your father played the saxophone in nightclubs back in Hong Kong, over the yellow sea. From the stories you have told me over our eighteen years together, I know you had longed to be with him. To have Frank Sinatra pat you on the head, give you a Coke. And when your father went off in the night with his friend Gloria, you could have gone, too, and sat under the table near Gloria's long, cool legs. Perhaps right at this moment you are still longing to be with him?

You learned about betrayal while holed up in the Bela Vista Hotel.

Leaving the film director, we ride the jet-cat back to Central, skimming over the mysterious currents of the South China Sea, skirting a scuttled pirate boat. You are like a patient lost in intensive care, my presence like a butterfly in a bottle. In the silence I imagine the relief if you would just throw me a line.

∽

From the huge glassed room in the university staff club, high above Central, I can see the New Territories and, beyond Lion Rock, the line of high-rise buildings snaking around Kowloon Bay. The rain of the last few days has stopped and the sky is blindingly blue.

There are two people sitting by the window. It is as though the girl is absorbing the whiteness of the huge air into her body. It fills her and empties her at the same moment. She is crying silently now, shedding her grief in waves, leaning her head over the plate so that it catches the fluid, leaving her face dry. She has done this before.

The man is one of the academic staff. Older. He doesn't move until he suddenly looks away from her like someone who has seen a car swerve away too late and now, in his cognac, suspects veins of blood.

She blows her nose on the serviette and I move to speak to her, but you place a hand gently on my arm.

He's ditching her, you say, with an authority that stills me.

∽

It is Gravesweeping Day. Chung Yeung. Mid-October now.

We are catching a taxi to the other side of the island. The lecturer in Romance languages lives in Celestial Towers on Sha Wan Drive. A van appears around the corner near the cemetery. As it swings out to avoid us, a coffin slides to one side in the back.

At the top of the tower her apartment hangs over the harbour. We stand on a tiny balcony. Far below I can see the university pool where I often swim. The other guests include the film director in a white suit. When he sits down I see that he wears no socks. There is an Australian journalist. A playwright. A Melbourne academic. The Filipina maid brings us drinks. I ask her name. She says it quietly: Flor. And there is a softness to her eyes as she moves away.

Dr Rose, the lecturer in Romance languages, is dressed in cream linen. Her hair is dark red. All the strands are the same length and fall from the crown of her head to a point one inch above her shoulders, a perfect, smooth helmet. She looks to be, like me, in her early forties. She's the sort of woman who always places a jacket over her shoulders, never puts her arms through the sleeves. She sits this way with her legs gracefully crossed, and scoops back the hair from her forehead with manicured hands.

We are speaking of the expatriate community in Hong Kong and the exploitation of young students by washed-up English academics well past their use-by dates.

The journalist laughs. Everyone is having an affair with everyone else in Hong Kong.

Are you? asks the playwright.

Oh, I would, but no one has asked me!

I learn later that the journalist has committed herself to Hong Kong, having married a Chinese. She is the only one of those present tonight who will be staying on after 1997. All the others about the dinner table will slip away at midnight like the governor.

It is at this moment that the lecturer in Romance languages presents the rose-petal ice-cream. She tells Flor to bring it to me first and Flor places it carefully before me on the table. The petals curl and fall to the plate. I am the honoured guest.

The lecturer in Romance languages has been working on the biography of a French woman who wrote novels in the 1940s. She speaks of the careful research, the bundles of letters.

One finds these love letters and you know that no one else has read them since they were first written, first read. The excitement of that. One unpacks the language. It's seriously thrilling.

You pick up a glass of wine and hold it to your lips without drinking for a moment.

I tracked down a niece who knew a bit. A vamp from way back. Drove out to the farm to interview her. She was one of those people who arrange their books on the shelves according to size. You know, the big books with the big books and the little books with the little books. She didn't trust me. Thought there were things that were best left unwritten. I got it out of her in the end, though.

As the lecturer in Romance languages speaks I become a little restless and suggest that the difficulty is in the choosing of the story. In writing a biography you really invent it yourself, don't you?

No. There are the facts. So and so did this. Or that.

Isn't there always the other story? Perhaps the more interesting one is the one that remains unwritten. The alternative story.

The playwright sitting beside me speaks then.

I came home one evening to the welcome of the green eye blinking in the dark. It was a message on the answering machine. That's the way he did it after fourteen years. I pressed the play button and heard him tell me that it was over. He had met someone else. Then there were just the beeps.

The lecturer in Romance languages holds her breath, leans forward to receive the end of the story.

I didn't ever see him again.

It is a little dangerous now. The playwright's grief threatens to spill onto the table. So the talk turns to plagiarism back in Australia, lawsuits, a play about dogs. The film director tells me more of his life story. Unconsciously his hands move to locate the cameras as he speaks.

I study the table on which Dr Rose keeps the precious boxes she has collected from around the world. Over dinner, while Flor is in the kitchen, she tells us she has given the maid a week's notice. Flor had thrown away an ancient manuscript painted on silk that she had found on Hollywood Road just the other day and bought for her lover in Paris. The maid had mistaken it for a piece of rubbish and put it down the chute.

After coffee Dr Rose gives a little cough, and turns her gaze upon you.

Philippe, I have asked you here for a reason. A proposal to put to you. Now that the biography is finished I'm at a loose end.

You put down your glass.

I thought I'd start on yours.

You look directly at her now, your eyes widening. She glances at me, sees the expression in my eyes. A little smile at this, then she looks about her.

I've made a start. The material you've already told me will be useful. I've taken notes from our conversations. But I want the rest. The whole thing.

You are about to be reeled in on the sure hook of narrative. This time it is you who silently smiles, and it seems there is nothing to be said, nothing to be done. Touching your lips to the white damask serviette like a priest after tasting the wine, you lean towards the lecturer in Romance languages to speak about the beauty of thought. With the Melbourne academic, I discuss the best ways to encourage possums to leave a house.

It is the end of the evening. People are standing and farewelling each other. You and the lecturer in Romance languages are looking at the view one last time. Out to the dark sea of sky. Across the room your backs are to us for a moment. You lean down and kiss her upon the neck.

As we descend Celestial Towers in the elevator, I am remembering the time when you and I saw rescue workers dredging a river in France. The ambulance cruising along the edge, waiting for the body to rise to the surface like a dead fish. I am also thinking of the differences between the word *neck* and the word *throat*.

I am washing out with the tide.

Days later I take the minibus to Lower Albert Road down to the Fringe Club, next to the Foreign Correspondents' Club. I call out, *Yau lok*, and the driver brakes for me to get off. You have arrived before me. The lecturer in Romance languages has had her hair cut.

I am seriously in love. That hairdresser was quite a number, she laughs.

With his guitar, the singer in the corner croons: *Mama says, it's all right to dream.*

It is the end of October. I return one evening to the flat to meet you as we had arranged. You are not there. I pick up the phone but do not know where to call. It is late when the phone finally rings.

Isabelle, I'm so sorry for not ringing you sooner. After my class I caught the boat to Lamma Island to have a look. I came across this bar and I've been having a beer with a whole lot of Germans playing mah-jong. I've missed the last boat back.

Your voice is fading on the phone. I guess I'll have to spend the night here somewhere. Don't worry about me.

When you hang up, the long, heavy night awaits me. I look up Lamma Island in my guidebook. It lies off the southern side of Hong Kong, across the East Lamma Channel. Outside I hear waves of jackhammers, the brakes of buses on Conduit Road, imagine the fall of population down to Victoria Harbour. In another hemisphere our house would be standing in crystal air, sharp as a currawong call.

The airconditioner kicks in above the ceaseless noise of the deconstruction, reconstruction of Hong Kong. I lie in the hold of its roar, which is like the scream of CX-100 on its night flight from Sydney to Hong Kong.

Someone brushes against the door. Then a sound from the next flat. I see the shadow of a crane in the night. There is perhaps a death somewhere. I think that death is simply the sound, through a wall in a foreign city, of a body slipping on a porcelain bath.

The bell is hanging silently from the roof outside the window like a black tear. I pull the curtain back, lean on the desk and take a photograph of it.

Then I turn on the lamp and write in my exercise book so that the scratching of my Chinese pen keeps me company. The pen in my hand is ready to face the teeth in the night, the bug-eyed bully that fear is. To write in the spaces created by your absence. But the hours are too long before me. I am restless in a restless city. I seek distraction.

I enter the night, making my way down through the crowds to Temple Street, past snakes in glass jars, the *Famous English-Speaking Fortune Teller*, the readers of faces who divined you from the partition of your brow, the fall of your cheek. Joss sticks smudge the air.

On the MTR a woman leaps, yelling, onto the train. She walks stiff-legged to the end of the carriage, where she folds her arms across her breast, her face averted from the crowd. There she stands trembling with rage as I leave the train at Tsimshatsui and join the human wave under caves of buildings with bamboo lines of washing like signals on schooners at sea. Signals of distress.

Finding the cool of the Ocean Terminal, I wander along a never-ending glitter of shops called the Silk Road: Venice, Istanbul, Baghdad, Teheran, Samarkand and Tashkent. The madder, indigo and saffron silk are mixed with the perfume of spices and the translucence of glass.

A tall, shaven-headed shopkeeper notices me standing before his shop filled with rolls of silk, and comes to the door. His shirt is perfectly white. He beckons me inside and begins to lay out silk upon a polished desk, taking my hand and placing it upon the material as if I am a blind person.

We have everything here, everything you could possibly desire, Madam.

And I wish that it could be so.

This is the paj. It can be used for anything at all, and here, the twill silk, the queen of silks. It has a nice sheen but doesn't sparkle too much. Not too gaudy. There is the velvety texture of the crepe de chine; there is the douppion, tussah, shantung, noil, the heavy, sensual charmeuse, and honan. Notice the colour blooming on this pongee.

Captured here by his words, I remain a few more moments.

My grandfather was a Russian émigré who fled to Paris and earned his living making men's silk handkerchiefs. So silk is in my family. And here I am, in Hong Kong.

He tells me that the Chinese judged their silk by its whiteness, its softness and fineness. They made damasks of all kinds and all colours: striped satins and the black satins of Nanking, watered moirés. To give the sheen to *tcheou tse* taffeta they used the fat of a freshwater seal called *kiang tchu*, the river pig.

He is still wanting to speak to me, but I must go.

Outside the Ocean Terminal a cruise liner, the *Pisces*, has docked and a crowd is swelling towards it, cries of *Aiya!* flying up into the air. I push through them to reach the ferry terminal, past a sign advertising a harbour cruise and, as an enticement: *Two Soft Drinks and a Vegetarian Meal.*

On the Star Ferry, I rise and fall in the opaque air, resting in its moving heart. The ferry passes an island of cranes. The boats of the egg people hang in water as the *Celestial Star* groans softly, rumbles into reverse, leans, moans to the wooden pylons slick with wet and oil in the night lights. Ferries all named for stars: *Lone, Morning, Meridian, Golden, Northern, Shining, Day* and *Silver*.

I stop in at the Mandarin Oriental for tea, and see purple stocks held in a vase against black marble, an old man in a long, grey gown giving a young woman a ring in a box. His glance at me tells me that I am his witness. The other couple. Young, American. Some difficulty there. She suddenly lifts the cigarette lighter up to his face. Snaps on the flame. He has no cigarette.

Outside again, I am assaulted by the heat.

The Stanley Ho pool is down Bisney Road past the cemetery and the olive mountain sprayed with concrete. In the pool I part water with my hands, gaze across Victoria Harbour to brightly lit tankers floating on the dark face of the sea. In the swell of the pool my smooth limbs meet silken water. Against my face and through my hair it sets me gleaming. My strong brown arms throwing off drops, as they did when, as a fifteen-year-old, I swam in the Tarwin River with my younger sister, Madeleine.

Outside the pool I wait for the bus, and when I climb aboard and sit down beside a woman it is Flor, the sacked maid.

She recognises me and smiles.

The bus winds past the hospital.

I'm going home, she says. First I must see my friends, then I'm going home.

I don't know whether she means her home in Hong Kong or the Philippines.

The bus terminates at Edinburgh Place beside the dockyards and the barracks.

Flor takes my arm. I'd like you to meet my friends, she says. It is as if we are allies.

She leads me to Statue Square and it is like entering an aviary. There is a sound like a thousand starlings. The Filipina maids are perched everywhere in the night. A flock. High-pitched exchanges of news from home. Flor sits on the pavement outside the GPO. Crowds flow towards the ferries. There is a man selling round, golden patties that he is flipping on a griddle.

Flor sits beside a large cardboard box that her friend, Connie, has been keeping safe for her. It is open. She is removing things from her bag. She places her clothes, her precious things in the box: the green silk happy coat, postcards and pictures of Victoria Harbour at night. She places a piece of brown paper between two layers of clothing, and puts the bribes for the customs officials on top. She addresses it to Manila. It will travel ahead of her. Flor is going home.

I imagine the telephone ringing unanswered in the lecturer in Romance languages' empty flat. Soon there will be dust on the little boxes. Grime accumulating. Without Flor there will be a steady decline. She tells me how angry she is, how she threw the map out accidentally because she thought it was a piece of garbage, a piece of brown paper. Dr Rose should not have sacked her for such a thing. She has a child to support. Her eyes grow large with the telling.

I sit with Flor and Connie, who wears a bright pink shirt. Flor sets a radio on the ground. She speaks quickly, ceaselessly, to Connie, who cares for the children of an English couple in Sandy Bay. Then she turns to me.

I would like you to meet my daughter.

So we take the MTR to Kowloon Bay. Here there are hanging pigs' corpses, bubbling pots on street stoves, trays of plastic, beeping watches. She leads me up some stairs to a door that has bars across it. There is a beautiful sound falling through the bars. When Flor opens the door I see a young girl of about nine. She sits straight-backed at a piano that must have taken Flor's savings for years. As we come in she glances around, but Flor gestures to her to continue.

Her black hair falls neatly and her white shirt hangs from thin shoulders. She plays 'The Swan' without moving her body. When she is finished she quietly accepts my praise and brings me mooncake to eat. I drink iced chrysanthemum tea poured from a can. The child plays again as I eat and drink and my fingers remember playing my mother's Lipp piano so many years ago. The heat radiates from the street, the pavement below, and a fan shifts the warmth around the room. I hear shouting in the flat next door. When the child plays there is a great stillness within me. I rest there, listening, for a long time.

It is very late when I return to the flat and sleep with the sea-roar of the airconditioner screaming above the buzz of the dragonflies and the screeching sulphur-crested white cockatoos outside in the courtyard.

I dream of sitting on the edge of the fish pond outside your office. An old woman sweeps flowers from the flame tree into little heaps. Piles of flames lie at my feet. I am sweating and lower my head into the cool water, brush against a fish nest on a ledge, feel the tusk of a sleeping fish. Fish feed on my face. I throw in a coin and kill a goldfish. It floats to the surface, belly up.

Your return long after dawn awakens me from this dream. You sit on the bed and tell me the rest of the story:

After I rang you I asked the boy at the bar where I could stay the night. When he'd finished washing the glasses, he took me down along a path to the Concerto Inn, where he said he worked during the day. There was a bright lamp at the door. It looked a fragile construction of bamboo. I could see several storeys and repeated roofs, steeply pitched, with projecting, upturned eaves and ridges of coloured tiles. Inside, just opposite the entrance, there was a carved screen wall. There was no one about. He led me through passageways to a red chamber where he said I could stay the night. One whole wall was constructed of a panel of windows and mirrors. There was a bed and a basin. I lay down and slept until the sun woke me. I couldn't find anyone around, so I left some money for him on the table and made my way to the dock. I was the only passenger aboard the ferry that brought me back to Hong Kong…

Your story told, you hunt the lizard from the bathroom, and take a shower. You sleep even though the sun is high, and as I look at your sleeping face I know that it is only latitude that binds you to me now.

~

Later, we meet the lecturer in Romance languages at the Red Pepper in Causeway Bay.

I missed the ferry and got stranded on Lamma Island.

She glances at me. Her lips part a little.

A very silly thing to do. Shall we have coffee at the Park Lane?

You speak with her of Shanghai until I long to go there.

Later, when we are alone, your language is a gesture pointing at something. You are speaking of *unpacking* language: a word you would use in a sentence about a suitcase, luggage and travelling, but not about ideas.

I struggle to remember where I have heard the word recently. I sense my own bags there in the corner. It is as though you are waiting for me to pick them up. To go.

~

The next day brings a Shanghai surprise. Odelia Lee's nails are burnished sienna. On her computer they seek me a room at the Peace Hotel on the Bund in Shanghai. She wears a brocade of kingfishers' feathers. She hands me my passport with the visa for China, the plane ticket, the voucher for the hotel. I will listen to the jazz band in the lobby there. See the couples dancing in Shanghai. I will watch the women on bicycles with their white gloves. Visit the museum off the Bund before catching the plane back to Hong

Kong after a few days. You have said you have too much work to do to come with me. So I will travel to Shanghai alone.

Before leaving Shanghai, I will visit the market early in the morning to buy a small wooden box for Dr Rose, who has shown me the brochures on Shanghai, and who sits beside me now telling me about the beauty of Shanghai, getting me such a good rate because Odelia Lee is a student of hers at the university.

⌒

It is the Sunday before I am to leave for Shanghai. I knock on your office door, open it. You and the lecturer in Romance languages are dancing. There is no music but you are dancing an odd literary dance. I stop suddenly and step backwards. Hit by the pane of glass between reality and fiction. I see that you are in the thrall of expert knowledge. I am an Outer Barbarian in the Celestial Empire. Overbalancing a little in my own awkward dance, I back away.

The lecturer in Romance languages steps delicately into the jacaranda shoes that lie near your desk. Walks past me out the door in her jacaranda dress. Under the hand that you have put to your mouth, you dampen your paper lips. Your eyes slide from mine, then you look at me again. In the corner of my eye is the sofa.

We leave the office. There is a pillar I stand beside. There is the knowledge that I should move away from your news for my own safety. I remain. I sweat.

Your hands are in your pockets. An announcement: I am falling in love.

Your words like bombs dropped from a plane passing over-head. The explosions in the territory of my heart will come later.

Falling of hopes, of my voice, of a shot bird, of leaves, of rain. From grace.

So I ask whether you will stay. With me. You grin, or perhaps it is a grimace against the Chinese sun in your eyes, and say that you can't. You have found someone. You have to find out. Your eyes move like dark birds across your face. You tell me that the story has changed. You have rewritten the future. It does not include me. There is exclusion in your voice. The husky note of betrayal. An old story, after all.

Falling, falling.

There are four days after that. I walk about until there is blood in my shoe, go to the library and sit before an open book. There is something I have to do but I cannot remember what it is; I am like water forgetting to freeze.

The nights move slowly. You talk of what your new life will be like, gently telling me that you will travel the world with the lecturer in Romance languages. You contemplate the perfection of your coupling. While you are speaking, I see only the absence of grief. When I am alone there is a sound coming from me. My eyes swell with hot fluid. It spews from me. I turn the airconditioner up high. No one can hear me.

One morning, I see Madeleine's back in the crowd boarding the Star Ferry. She has come to me. I hurry after her. Of course, it is not her.

You say grief is like an axe in a tree. As time passes the axe remains but the handle drops off. It gets better.

There is nothing else for me to do. When I ring Cathay Pacific to change my flight, I observe the relief in your face.

⌒

We take a car to Kai Tak for the late flight to Sydney. You drive. In my haste I leave a pair of my shoes behind. The cleaner waves them in the air after the car. Sweat drops between my breasts. There is no sound as the car swings past the high-rise and I sit stiffly on the seat, looking out the window. My eyes are bright with the anticipation of loss, my fingertips pressed to my mouth. My departure and the inevitability of it are two prongs of nausea. I bow forward in the seat. My head glances against the dashboard. You look uneasily at me, and press your foot on the brake gently. You turn off the engine and watch me. Reach your hand out to my forehead as you would to a child.

Easy, easy. As to an injured animal.

Soon I drag myself upright and hear the whistle of my breath, like the irritated scroop of a black cockatoo. You start the engine and wind the car back on to the road. I see a little blood on your hand, blood on the wheel.

You've hurt yourself.

No.

There's blood on your hand.

Yours.

You seem to be holding your breath. My hand rests on the vinyl seat. You place your hand upon mine and let it remain there until we arrive at the airport terminal.

As we wait in the Goodbye Cafe, I study the departure of others, caught in this moment's mirror. 'Rainy Night in Georgia' plays somewhere close and the notes are blown backwards by the raining wind. I pick up my bag and say, I guess this is it.

This is what?

The end.

The goodbye cafe

Katoomba.

The Three Sisters at Echo Point rise like lions in the sea, their shape repeated in the Sorensen cypresses that stand in scattering blue light across the mountains. A lifting mist reveals a tracery of ridges and ravines, fissures in the earth. There are cliffs that can throw a human cry from rock face to rock face, until, unheard, it drops into darkness.

Everywhere there is a falling away: rocks inclined towards the east have uplifted and fractured over millions of years. Heavy layers of yellow and brown sandstone are lined with shale. Volcanic necks lie on the north and the south sides of the ridge, giving a coastline to this sea of air. Jacaranda blue, only deeper.

In the steaming valleys the rainforest canopies spread on basalt caps, and mosses, liverworts, hornworts, lichens, fungi, orchids and ferns flourish in deep gorges. The dry sclerophyll forests, flecked with yellow wattle, lie along the ridge tops, the upper-valley slopes where houses have been built on thin, sandy soil. A place so raw, its inhabitants could wake to summer warmth but be lighting the fire by midday to escape misty rain.

Isabelle sits outside a house that burns in lamplight. White skins of tangled scribbly gums on the other side of the valley appear like smoke twisting through the bush. A distant train rattles as it pulls into Katoomba Station in Main Street, sounding like the shaking of teeth in an old dead head. She has told no one except Madeleine that she has returned from Hong Kong alone.

Isabelle turns her head from the bush and moves across the verandah to the door. Inside the room there is a piano, a desk under the window, and around it are walls of books, their covers evenly stacked in tight lengths, their reflections reaching into the night. The ceiling rises high above blades of double bookshelves; a body of books rises in every space around her. There are a heap of shoes on the floor, a tin trunk, boxes of books. She pauses and listens as an animal coughs in the night. The high poplars rub against each other as she takes a book from the top shelf. Inside Robert Lowell's *Notebook*, Philippe has numbered the names of the poet's ex-wives in careful script, each number like a hand grenade. Placing it in a box, she reaches again and finds the book of poems he bought in the heat of the tents in Adelaide and shyly offered to a towering Ted Hughes, who wrote in the flyleaf: *Hair by hair you might pluck a life bald.*

Working like this for several hours, Isabelle is slowly clearing the forest of books. At night, in the heat, she has been packing them for weeks, will pack them until the walls are scraped back to themselves. The night's choreography gives her days their shape and meaning.

Somewhere there is the dark voice of a dog.

Tonight she starts on the novels and finds slipped inside them the photographs Philippe used as bookmarks. As she gazes at the photographs she knows it will never be over.

1976. Isabelle and Philippe in Madeleine's room in the school in St Denis.

After their marriage they went travelling through Europe. Madeleine picked them up in a taxi from the Hotel Danube in the rue Jacob, where they had spent three nights listening to the wallpaper crumbling and had woken suddenly in the night when the American choir girls returned to the hotel. They were down on the street, at the door.

Happy Noo Year, Happy Noo Year, they called softly across the evening to each other, and for years afterwards, on each New Year's Eve, Philippe would kiss her neck and whisper to her at midnight in a soft American accent, and she would smile.

The next morning, as Philippe chatted to Madeleine in French, his mother's tongue, Isabelle arranged him against the dark drop cloth she had fashioned from her black winter coat hung by the window. His pipe sat on its side on the table.

For the cover of your first novel, she laughed as he rolled his eyes at Madeleine. Keep still.

He held his face to the darkness, and she took the picture.

~

1977. France.

Travelling to Fontainebleau with Madeleine and another teacher they always referred to as the Spaniard, they followed a road in a forest of straight-limbed trees brushed in narrow waves up to the low cloud. Rain waited to fall upon a tall, grey stone house that looked like a nest on the edge of the forest. In the gardens of the chateau were some yawning soldiers, hands on hips, scarlet cloaks spread. Three donkeys screamed at the train

29

running behind the chateau. In the *jardin anglais*, an old man sat on a seat intently focused on the sway of the swan on the pond. Or perhaps he was asleep.

Through the trees a horse kicked up leaves and warmed the air with its steaming dung. An officer was exercising his big bay, his eyes flickering over them without interest as the Spaniard took the photo.

On the way back, the Spaniard's laugh in the back seat was like the twanging of a guitar. As Philippe's eyes met Isabelle's and Madeleine's, the three of them smiled at each other in antipodean collusion.

After driving about for an hour, trying to find the school, Madeleine finally stopped on an overpass in fog and the Spaniard, gathering his coat about him, climbed out of the car and stood on the road in the night lit by broad, searching sweeps of orange light.

Where are we? Isabelle asked.

We're lost, said Philippe.

1976. Philippe and the boat in the country.

Madeleine must have taken this early picture, because her writing is on the back. He was young, his hair long. She must have held the camera into the breeze; Isabelle can hear the click in the rush of open air. There were miles of brown water. After the picnic on the shore, Isabelle and Philippe had fallen in the warm water fully clothed and the boat flapped beside them like a pelican. The hills were brown behind the sails, the sky white with the last of the Australian summer heat. They rolled in the dam with each other, their faces stretched with laughter.

When they were aboard again, the breeze picked up and Philippe turned the boat until the wind was directly behind them. He loosened the sheets, then let them all the way out, and the sails swung free. Isabelle stretched out on her back and felt the warm water sliding along the edge of the boat, streaming over her arm. As Philippe held the rudder steady they ran back towards the shore, goosewinging, with the sound of metal clinking on the mast. And they sailed back like that, happy with the expectation of being carried home on the sure evening wind.

～

1982. Philippe and the dog.

It was early morning and raining lightly. They descended into the blue-gum forest that lay far beyond the house, and ran together with the dog over the sodden earth along the floor of the valley, past waratahs flaring suddenly before them like the red burst of king parrots flying through the green.

They ran for miles. There was no one else, just the companionship of the breath and the dog between them running sideways, her tongue lolling with each step, then the climb at the end to South Head, where Isabelle bent down and drank from the pool of water with the dog.

～

1992. The house in Katoomba.

Built from golden cypress pine on the side of a valley, it had a silvery green roof. They slept high up in the house below a pane of glass that gave an eye to the night. In the morning the house creaked in response to the warming air and they would wake to the gulping cry of a swooping currawong. Rising, they would step out onto a small deck so high above the tree line that parrots flew beneath them, squeaking with the sound of two branches rubbing together in a breeze. On the deck was a table where they drank tea and leaned over the bow of the house set upon the grey swell of an ocean of eucalypts.

They moved into the house one June day years ago, away at last from the heat of the city. At night they walked through the cemetery with the dog, Philippe sniffing up the snowy air like cocaine. Once they sat in the darkness on the verandah, listening to Borodin's *Nocturne* at midnight under the bright, cold sky, the dog at their feet as she told him a story: A tall woman was caressing her husband's feet, stroking him to death. They did not catch her. Caresses leave no trace. It was a slow death and he died with his foot in the air, and his lips folded in.

1955. Hong Kong.

In the dim photo of Philippe in the flat, the dog is bigger than he is. His wide, serious face is looking at his toy aeroplane in the corner of the picture, carefully lined up with the cars on the windowsill. There are a lounge, a television, some chairs.

Although she had carried that photo of him as a child with her for years, she wasn't quite sure why it moved her so.

1976. Philippe.

She took this photograph in February, not long after they first met. There is the clean line of the cheek, the eyes averted. Her fingers touch his cheek. There is a hollow in the skin here, a small strawberry birthmark in the shape of a dog. His eyes are green, with hazel patches in some lights. She holds the photograph as if tempted to lower her face against it, to glean the scent of him. For Isabelle, in this moment, there is nothing but his eyes of woven glass and the slow pulse of memory. He is telling her the story of his family. They are young and it is the first time she has heard this story. A bottle of Mateus sits between them on the table. His fingers are brushing at the label, finding the rift where it lifts a little from the cool glass. She is listening to him and watching his hands, like birds in their shape, flashing between trees.

It was raining when they met; it was raining as the dark trees silently observed their path between the house and the car, and inside the warm enclosure the car made there was Rakhmaninov. First it was twilight, then much later when they returned it was the falling darkness that he stopped with his upturned palms. He whispered Yeats to her: *I have spread my dreams under your feet; tread softly because you tread on my dreams*. And he took her head in one hand and drew it to that place between his shoulder and throat and she felt the warm, soft brushing of lips upon her eyelids, sealing them against a future she would not want to see. Did he know it even then?

⌒

Isabelle drops the photograph and opens the lid of the piano carefully. She sits on the stool and runs her hands across the keys, tapping them with her long fingers, remembering when she was very young and her mother still played. But when the notes begin to form meaning their sounds grate upon her. Sharply she closes the lid and the strings shiver in the air. She turns her back on the piano and stacks the photographs in a box. Then she picks up more books, cold stones in her hands, and climbs the stairs to the bed in the room that hangs like a kite over the eucalyptus forest. She lies there watching the blue backs of flies. She hears the sound of a hubcap from the wheel of a car on the highway, spinning off into the night.

Her bed is her grave. On it lies a heavy body of books, the revolver that had been handed down through the French side of Philippe's family to him, and a pile of Madeleine's letters. She lies against these things, her grave goods, and falls into sleep as into a dark pool below her, sleeping deeply, entombed with a copy of the book of the dead, fully clothed in a green dress and boots. Her eyes closed to her journey, she is studying the map of it in her sleep. Sweat leaks from her body as she sleeps like a creature that has had a net thrown around it in the sea. Her sleep is like a drowning, a slow slipping away under water. Last night she woke in the dark, swung out of bed, hitting her bones on the cupboard. He was lost in the darkness below and she must reach down and grasp his hand and pull him up from the black water lapping at her feet.

The moon outside the window is an old one and she is the sad wife, sleeping as though her pillow has been dipped in a bucket of ether. She doesn't move. She will wake with her head still turned to the window, listening to the sound of the wind in the eucalypts, like the sound of waves reaching at the shore, falling back, failing. She is a shipwreck, smashed on a reef of writing.

When she opens her eyes, it is because she hears the house speaking to her in the morning light, the wood bending, stretching, groaning like a boat on waves of heat. Below the house, the grass lies flat and the willows shake their heads of hair. A bird's line of flight crosses the stand of gums.

She lives day after day like this right through summer. For company, there are only the phone calls to Madeleine, and the dog, who stays close.

She thinks about telling people that Philippe has died in Hong Kong. It will be only Madeleine who she can bear to know the truth. She rehearses the story with Madeleine on the phone:

We ride this night on the *Celestial Star*. We sit at the rear on wooden seats polished by the passage of a million people. You can trace the brass star in the wood with your finger. The two middle-aged Americans who sit in front of us absorb me and I think he is kissing her foot. I lean forward to see him carefully clipping her toenails, and turn back to Philippe to laugh. But he is gone. He is falling from the back of the ferry in a moment carved in the air.

His arms stretch out to me. His glasses are slipping on his nose. He is falling into the Fragrant Harbour. As he flies, he parts the black water and his body makes a dark hole that is quickly filled. (Did I look away to see the lights of Kowloon in the soft, soft dark, and turn back to find you gone?) I hear five bells across the sea. A cleaving apart.

The next morning the *South China Morning Post* said: *At 7.30 pm last night a forty-three year old man man fell from a Star Ferry into Victoria Harbour as it made its way from Central. An extensive search of the area was unable to locate him.*

A body dipping into the sea.

As her voice fails, Madeleine says, I'll come.

From the verandah, the dog listens to her whispering to Madeleine. The dog waits for him still, but somehow Isabelle knows better than to wait. She gazes at herself in the mirror, at the green dress hanging loosely, shocked to discover that her grief has manifested itself so clearly in her face. Taking a pick down to the creek, she hooks into the earth and plants sentinel agapanthus under trees that stand like temples over her bent figure. She fills the holes with dirt and the heat dries her face. Like a Western red cedar, Isabelle is rotting from the inside, necrosing; slowly the blood in her body dries to a rusted mark.

Once again, the night swings deeply across the valley, bringing more than just the absence of light. She dreams there are people at the door who are knocking on the wood. A rescue party hovers in a helicopter out here in the South China Sea. The house groans and rolls in the gale like a scuttled boat. The wind is sucking at the walls. The beams stretch and strain as it rolls for days; its mast is broken and trails in the sea. In the dark wind outside, she hears the sound of a murderous typhoon, the call of the whale far beneath her. The house rubs its back against a bony reef, a skeleton in the sea.

She wakes when a crack of thunder parts the air, and rain falls in. She lies still, as if carved. She thinks of the leap from Honeymoon Lookout, the cliffs of fall.

Feeling a worm in her heart moving, she hears the scream of the black cockatoo in the pines, like the bellow of a horse gone mad and in need of a bullet. She thinks of her ovaries with their eggs, an aviary—and delicate birds' eggs shrivelling there. She is like the bride who wakes on her wedding day with a beard. It is only the light coming through the stained-glass window above the bed that gets her into the day.

She fills a vase with tears and it is dark again. Every evening she sleeps in the green dress and boots. Night after night there are Chinese colours in her brain and she forgets to breathe.

Very late one night, she walks out onto the top deck and listens to the night noises, the voice of the wind. She climbs up on to the table and stands high above the trees, looking down to the hanging swamp. She draws herself up, gathers herself from her centre, and prepares for flight, a dive into the pool of night, the well of darkness below.

The telephone rings.

She freezes as though caught in the act of a crime. Impatiently she waits for the phone to fall silent. It rings and rings. It does not stop. The dog begins a frenzy of barking.

Defeated, Isabelle climbs from the table and walks slowly down the stairs to the telephone. She picks up the receiver and hears her sister's voice coming from far away. She murmurs across the seas to Madeleine in Paris. This barren crust of earth, these harsh trees and rocks of Katoomba, have become embedded in her heart. She will seek an end in the beauty of some other place. As Madeleine speaks, Isabelle thinks of that strangely shaped faraway tree of their childhood, the carruba tree.

No, don't come, she says to Madeleine. I will go to Ravello.

A good end point, she thinks, and, as if led on by the luxurious rolling sound of her own words, she continues.

I will go to Ravello. Meet me there?

～

But time is unmoving, like a stone, and she remains. The cold edges in under her door.

Lighting the fire for company, to hear it move, to feel its arms of heat, she scratches at her breast to get at the ache. She recognises the silence. It is the quiet despair of her mother, and she has become her own mother.

She runs through the bush, the trees moving in the wind like disturbed spiders. Above her a kookaburra sits observing her from its perch on a dead branch, a small fish hanging from its beak. She wears Philippe's shirt, his boots. There is a rawness to her organs that finds a skin in his clothes. She runs through scribbly gums, encoded writing carved into their trunks, white like the trees of the brain, with arms of blanched bone. A graffiti of branches scratches at her as she passes. A flock of black cockatoos clouds the sky. Her feet slide on rocks. The stones and leaves on the ground have faces.

The dog follows at a distance, accustomed to Philippe's shirt with his smell moving through the scrub, but not this cold keening in the wind.

As she runs, there is her dialogue with grief and she says aloud: I am in Katoomba. It is Friday. She speaks so that the past will not take her. Throw back its head, hold her upside down above its mouth, drop her in and swallow her whole.

Looking back up from the hanging swamp, she sees the wooden house where it perches above the eucalypt valley: a boat, a church, a violin. During the day it moves, expands and breathes, pressing soft cypress perfume into the air.

Night after night she dreams that her heart is sleeping in a hollow of dirt beneath the house. It waits, shivers. Some days she sees it sitting in a gutter, bent double, its hand over its mouth. She forgets to feed it and it grows thin and bony.

She hears a rat scratching in the room, but when she opens her eyes sees that it was just the rain. She walks out into rain and an aria of currawong song.

To clear her head of the dream, she chops wood for hours, then sits inside and watches the mist coming into the house through the open window. The past rolls in to her living room with the cloud. Isabelle tries to light the fire without him. Three times it fails. She weeps as the light in his eyes dies and she knows that we don't know what life takes us to. The events in Hong Kong were like a coal train in the night. No lights. Just the moon catching the side of the last truck. She was blind. She should have seen it coming. There was one detail, merely pointed at, that she missed, and so lost the whole.

～

Philippe could never settle with one meaning, so there had been nothing for her to grasp, except the falling night as he surfed on the swell of language, reaching for happiness, writing in red ink on polished paper, naming his gods with each thick downstroke, thin upstroke. She can see him holding his breath as he wrote onto the empty space of the page.

What is a wound, she thinks, if not a longing for language?

Philippe was a man who selected his dog according to how difficult it would be to bury; he placed his affections carefully, like a priest setting the bread and wine on the altar. Isabelle learned restraint, silence, never to speak of an experience because then it couldn't be written about, and that was the worst thing.

So nothing really existed or happened. His dialogue was with the page; he kept it for the page. Everything was for the page. He wrote with three books open in front of him on his desk, greedy for the seduction of words. He wrote in heavy woollen clothes, sometimes with a scarf about his throat and his breath a white banner because he had forgotten to stoke the fire and it had died down. When Isabelle came into the house just a cough told her that he was there. She would relight the fire, smelling the wood and ash on her frozen hands, and see that his thoughts were elsewhere, and he was falling over some sort of edge, giving himself up to the jazz that played on the radio—dark, muddy music. He was a scriptor in his scriptorium, scooping up the cream of language as it came to the top. Philippe took their life, soaked it in lime, scrubbed away all trace of flesh and hair, dried it, and scraped again with a knife blade, then polished the surface to give parchment to write on.

He was afraid he would lose his voice if people came and talked about his work, so there was no one. Only Madeleine's letters from Paris. Isabelle played endlessly on the Lipp piano she had inherited when her parents died. Sometimes she'd glance up to see Philippe listening with his eyes closed.

There was simply his sleeping early, in summer to escape the heat, in winter to escape the darkness, dreaming that writing would save him from a life that was a calligram: he was the shape of his texts. He did not notice her love for him, his gaze being upon the words.

Then one night, alone by the fire, she started writing on scraps of his yellow paper as he slept in the room above her. Guiltily she put down her pen and fed the fire, watching the ink grow dark and the words curling up into the chimney and floating out over the hanging swamp, the stand of scribbly gums. After that Isabelle would find herself surreptitiously writing letters to herself.

The film director's visit was an intrusion. He rang to say he had read the synopsis of the spy novel Philippe was writing, and wanted to make it one of his next projects. He said he could meet up with them when they went to Hong Kong. He and Philippe could choose locations together. He thought Macau would be right for the love scenes. The decay. That lost city feel about it. There was a particular hotel, the Pousada de Sao Tiago. It was

set like a bunker in the side of the hill. They could meet him
there. He insisted on coming up to Katoomba on the train to pay
a visit; accustomed to the eccentricities of genius, he wouldn't
take no for an answer.

So they took him down through the hanging swamp and up
the other side of the valley to the high heath, to show him the
waratahs. It was building to a storm, and when it broke the rain
came at them in great sweeps. It struck the sweat on the back of
the film director's neck. He struggled for breath as they hastened
back to the house, the dog running ahead searching for lizards,
snakes, anything she could hunt down. Django Reinhardt's
'Daphne' was on the radio. The film director rubbed his hair dry
with the towel Isabelle had given him.

You know, Philippe, your life is an observed one. Not a lived
one. You need some passion in your life. You can't write about
what you haven't known, he said.

Isabelle paused a moment over the coffee she was making
and looked across at the film director, then at Philippe. She
looked into his eyes. His lips parted a little as if he were to say
something. Always it seemed that he was about to say something. But he never did. He gave a stiff little smile and said
nothing.

After that he took longer trips to the city. She realises now
that he was researching the art of betrayal, writing his spy novel,
telling himself stories of passion, assuming another of the multi-
plicities of self that he kept stored away like honey in a glass jar.
All this time he was intently writing about fragmentation and
collapse. His despair bloomed like a black flower, and she could
smell it in the mornings, when she woke beside him.

Tell me a story, she said once in winter when she was ill and
lay in bed.

41

He gently told her about Russian forests and loss until she slept in his arms and woke to find the fever gone.

Sometimes he lay on the black couch in his black jumper in the long late afternoons. The worst times. His eyes were often closed and it was like a sentence. The unrelenting pressure of it pushed down upon him like a wool press, squeezing out life, love.

Anhedonia, he murmured.

She looked it up in his dictionary while he slept.

When she bent down to him lying there, she heard something else.

Australia.

The darkness plagued him until his heart had become a walled city, and Isabelle wondered if she were, after all, the cause of it. Perhaps he had caught it from her, as she, the unwitting carrier, had caught it from her mother.

There was just the dog, as loyal as Feather had been, always with him on his wild walks, the miles he ran to escape the plague, which came without warning. It was like the beating of rain across a valley: she could hear it coming, drumming its advance, long before she could see it, or feel it.

Once he opened his eyes for a second and said that he had to remain silent to write, but, for Isabelle, reading the silence was like trying to decipher hieroglyphics, a language stripped of vowels. It was incompatible with any alphabet she knew.

You don't attend to the thing, Isabelle. Drawing attention to love destroys it. You must not meet its gaze.

Such words became weapons at her throat. It was so clearly going wrong but she didn't know how or why. It was like wearing a dress inside out, so that the unravelling threads of her life were obvious to everyone else.

Something bursts in the toilet. She rings for help.

The plumber shuffles on the tiles in the bathroom, stirs the water of the cistern.

Australian made. Never last.

What should I do? asks Isabelle.

Got a replacement in the van. American, and more expensive. But you know where you are.

Ah, says Isabelle with a smile. I want to know where I am.

So he moves about the house, twisting and tapping pipes. There has not been another human being here for months. She is unused to movement about her, just the petal from a poppy falling from time to time, caught in the corner of her eye.

The plumber finishes his work.

There was this bloke who lived just down from here. Do you know about him?

Isabelle shakes her head.

His wife cleared out six months ago. Ran off with some other bloke. I did some work for him. Anyway, his aunt died and left him her five Rottweilers. He carried photos of the dogs in his wallet. I saw him in Katoomba Street one day, a few months back. We had a chat, and after a while he said he had to get back to the dogs. I heard later that one night he rang a taxi and ordered a case of beer. He drank it all at one go. When someone found his body a week later, the dogs had eaten bits of it.

Isabelle remembers the Rottweilers at the end of the road. She had been walking with the dog there one day when a Rottweiler appeared at the open window of the third storey of the wooden house. Then another dark head at a different window. The house was peopled with Rottweilers. They examined Isabelle and her dog silently, without moving. Suddenly one of the dogs yelped and disappeared. Isabelle quickened her pace, but they came out an open door and hurtled, with a third, a fourth, onto the road. Isabelle froze and pulled the dog close to her as the Rottweilers circled. She did not speak. Her blood stopped flowing and she remained paralysed for a few minutes, then moved off, pushing through them. And they stood looking at her as she and the dog continued down the road.

As Isabelle counts out his money, the plumber leans on the bench.

Nice spot, he says, looking to the fall of eucalypts hanging in the window, where tomorrow the fog will drift across her eyes like sleep, and a river of hyacinths will flood in spring.

⌒

Isabelle leaves her isle of the dead and ventures into Katoomba, past a bare tree flowering with cockatoos. Skeins of pigeons fly in a strange light, billowing out across the sky. Walking quickly past the Savoy, where she is known, she makes her way in to the darkness of the Paragon, where no one will notice her eating the edges of food among the tourists. She takes a booth at the back. No hummingbirds. They are off the menu today, she thinks she hears the waitress say.

A man across the room strokes a woman's chin and holds it between his thumb and forefinger like a sparrow. When Isabelle looks up again, the woman is taking into her mouth a piece of food from his proffered fork. Isabelle gets up suddenly and leaves without ordering.

Outside there is a woman waiting at the bus stop. She is old, with a beautiful face. Chinese. Tall. She wears a black woollen beanie and a long, dark coat that completely encloses her. It has a fluff of light brown fur at the collar. Her pale hand, holding a cigarette, emerges from the dark coat. She stares at Isabelle, and the bright sunlight around them is swallowed in grainy cloud.

Isabelle walks away, close to the shop windows. The wind catches her sideways as she crosses alleys. It is a wind that knows where ice and snow still lie, somewhere far to the south. She passes by her favourite bookshop, having no use for books now that the dyslexia of grief has struck her. Outside the shop, a young man, a shoplifter, screams like a rabbit as he is apprehended.

Alas!

Isabelle is startled.

Alas!

The young man is agitated, growing insistent, very ugly. When the woman from the bookshop appears at the door, he grasps her arm.

Alice.

She shakes off his hand, turns and walks back into the shop.

Leaving them, Isabelle walks home with fresh supplies of yellow paper. In a stretch of scribbly gums, a passing bus gives her a window of cypresses, black strokes in the purples and blues of receding shadow. Reaching the house, she takes the mail stuffed in the letterbox. A huntsman spider leaps away from her in fright. Her hands find a heavy, foreign letter from Madeleine. There is also one from Japan for Philippe. Inside it are the details of an Australian literary studies conference in Tokyo. A cheque for the airfare.

She will bank it.

That night she dreams that she is standing over Philippe's grave, murmuring, I am the sad wife. As it starts to rain,

Madeleine hands her an umbrella that she takes and swings over her head, showering the dark hole with confetti from some wedding long ago.

∽

Isabelle sits in the dentist's chair. His strong hands hold her jaw gently. As he waits for the anaesthetic to work, he moves into the next room and she can hear him playing a clarinet. He returns, finishes his work, and she sits up, blurred, sleepy with the music and his care.

Have a good winter.

She blinks, appreciating both his gentleness and the way he thought in seasons. As if he somehow knew that the frost would wait, axe in hand behind the door, to split her in two, drive her bones into the ground, and grind the pieces like glass with the heel of its foot. He's turned away now, and as she's leaning over the ceramic bowl, spitting beads of blood, he says it again: Have a good rinse.

∽

Over the summer, she has given away or sold all her possessions. But one evening, before the television goes, she sees Philippe on the screen.

Is he in Hong Kong? Is he in some other house, here in Australia?

He's standing beside an empty fireplace, resting his arm along the mantelpiece. He is wearing a white shirt, a tie. He looks prosperous. His hair has been cut short. As the interviewer speaks to him about the publication of his new novel, a doorbell is ringing somewhere off the screen. Isabelle knows what he is thinking about all this. About the camera, the lights. There is a slight shine to his forehead. He makes eye contact with the camera.

There is a camera here, he says, pointing at the truth, intent upon annoying the woman, refusing to play by the rules.

Writing, he says to the camera, you will abandon everything for that. You will betray everyone. All that matters is the work.

With the passing of time, Isabelle has understood that in Philippe's deception of her lay the truth.

⌒

Isabelle sits at Philippe's desk under the window, a net of trees against the sky. She takes up his pen and, in a pale voice, writes to Madeleine: *There is a floor in me, and I am lying on it.*

She has been packing the last of his papers and pens, which have lain there all this time, just where he left them. The pines groan. At her feet, the dog moves, folds her paws and tucks her head tightly into her tail to form a perfect circle. The cord of the blind hangs from the window in the precise way he had knotted it. In the months that she has been there alone, the tip of the pine tree outside has moved above the line of the windowsill.

She takes a piece of yellow paper. The black ink-drops on the page are like the shadow of a man. With her hand upon her chin, she writes a letter to the dead from the dead:

Dear Philippe
  In Katoomba I am kept alive in your protective custody.
I am something living, but very still. My arms were raised
on a corner in Hong Kong, as if to be taken in your arms to

dance. But my eyes are too big for my head. Your boots are too big for the bones in my feet. I have lost my concentration.

I place my shaven head upon the wooden bed. The wings of my shoulderblades, a swirl of bone down my back like folds in stone. A calligraphy of bone—skin over stone, cloth over bone. A skeleton after these months, my cells are shrinking like my liver in its cage. The organs inside my skin are playing my requiem.

In the dusk of morning light I stand, still as a Chinese warrior. Perhaps you have spun my hair for socks? Or are you on some South American street, living on my golden teeth?

I wait for winter with its quiet garden of snow…

Isabelle

She gathers together all the yellow pages that she has written upon—the yellow pieces of paper that have become her company—and adds them to the exercise book from Hong Kong. She slips it between the leaves of one of Philippe's unfinished manuscripts. It lies, in his careful script, on his writing desk, just as he had left it when they went to Hong Kong. She places her pages among the bones of his story, the flesh of his language.

As she lifts the papers, it is the shape of the words *The Concerto Inn* that first attracts her eye, like a familiar piece of music catching in the brain. Before she can stop herself, she reads the story and hears Philippe's voice telling her a familiar tale:

I asked the boy at the bar where I could stay the night. When he'd finished washing the glasses, he took me down along a path to the Concerto Inn, where he said he worked during the day. There was a bright lamp at the door. It looked a fragile construction of bamboo. I could see several storeys and repeated roofs, steeply pitched, with projecting, upturned eaves and ridges of coloured tiles. Inside, just opposite the entrance, there was a carved screen wall. There was no one about. He led me through passageways to a red chamber where he said I could stay the night. One whole wall was constructed of a panel of windows and mirrors. There was a bed and a basin. I lay down and slept until the sun woke me. I couldn't find anyone around, so I left some money for him on the table and made my way to the dock. I was the only passenger aboard the ferry that brought me back to Hong Kong...

Like a transparent structure superimposed over Philippe's story, Isabelle imagines another voice, not Philippe's. As the weight and density of the words shift, parallel lines finally converge in Isabelle's mind and she reads between them. She reaches her own vanishing point and apprehends a slippage in meaning, the resonance of another narrative. It is the lecturer in Romance languages whose voice she hears singing the *o* of *The Concerto Inn*. Philippe's words dematerialise and another story takes their place, as though a fragment of someone else's memory has drifted into Isabelle's mind:

How I tried to ignore Philippe's attentions, the *billets doux* at the conference in Guangzhou quoting Yeats: *I have spread my dreams under your feet; tread softly because you tread on my dreams.* He brushed my hand one night over dinner at the White Swan. He wrote me another note and had it delivered to my room. He impersonated a visiting Indian professor, but I knew who it was. He wrote to me: *Since the written word is*

49

*so much like a historical document, a hysterical formal amendment
to ways and behaviour, it would pleasure me greatly to request the
lascivious and lusty pursuits of my mind upon the joys of your body.
The fruits of our love shall not pass unrewarded in the annals of
time.*

I laughed then because we spoke the same language.
He was lost. He told me how he sat on the verandah in
Katoomba and drank whisky, his mother's revolver aimed at
his sadness. There was the warm breath that his language
was. It curled off his tongue. It wound around me and pulled
me closer. He could tell stories in the night, stories that were
like jewels, stories that were strung upon ideas so rare. So he
smuggled me in to him against my will. The intrigue of the
affair! Back in Hong Kong the hand upon my breast between
book-signings. The secrecy was divine.

Then Isabelle arrived in Hong Kong and it was even
better; his desire more urgent, driven by the betrayal he was
writing about. I was his reason now to chuck it in. He'd been
wanting to do it for a while. Had decided some time ago that
his life in Katoomba, Isabelle, had to go. Now that we had
found each other he could do it in one job lot. The garage
sale of his life.

We went to the Mandarin Oriental and I drank calvados.
There was a Portuguese band playing. He drank Mateus and
told me about his childhood in Hong Kong, being raised by
a Chinese amah who spoke only Mandarin, his early years
a tangle of different tongues. The awful betrayal of being
taken away from his French mother to Australia by his father
when he was eight and the only place he wanted to be was
Paris. And I can see him standing on some country train
platform, his tin trunk beside him, knowing that there would

be nothing up the line, down the line. I don't think he ever recovered from the culture shock of that.

In my flat I would tell Flor to have the day off. I think she knew why. I would put on my Gloria Estefan songs. The ones in Spanish. He would whisper into the intercom; then in my bed the whispering would become more urgent. His lips upon my throat until I felt like a long-necked Botticelli. The stroke of his hand along my thigh and the accumulation of flesh he gathered there. Afterwards he would go out on to my little balcony and write. I would make him coffee. He said it was the best writing he had ever done. I found little white cards all over the flat with quotations on them, like Italo Calvino's *There is no language without deceit*.

But they were merely moments, odd hours grabbed here and there. Until one evening I was sitting beside him at Jo Jo's bar in the Grand Hyatt in Wanchai as he rang Isabelle. I heard him tell her that he was stranded on Lamma Island and would stay the night somewhere.

He was hanging up the phone and smiling down at me on the stool beside him. My legs were crossed. I lifted my face slowly to his, and our eyes were like lovers walking towards each other on a street. I shifted my legs slightly. My hand lay at the place where the skirt ended on my thigh. Philippe placed his perfectly shaped hand upon mine.

We have the night, he said.

Isabelle is still. She does not breathe but sits holding in her hands the cold fact of Philippe as the architect of a carefully constructed deceit. Then she takes *The Concerto Inn*, thick now with her own dark story, and places it carefully in Philippe's trunk from Hong Kong. Gathering momentum, she packs all

51

the precious things he has given her over the last eighteen years: the love letters, the poems. Then all the things from his desk. She is sweating. The dog licks the sweat from her legs as she drags the trunk across the floor to the top of the back staircase, levers it down one step at a time. It slips and its weight pushes down on her. She falls backwards down the stairs and the trunk presses her against the floor. Looking up, she sees the perfect symmetry of her fall, and she is filled with anger. It is as if she has woken to the unfamiliar roar of a striking match.

The rage steams off her back like white frost burning in sun as she drags the trunk all the way under the house into the dark, where it lodges in the damp soil. The dog sniffs at it, picking up Philippe's scent, revelling in the memory of him. Turning away to the light at the open doorway, Isabelle spills outside again. Slams the heavy door shut. Closes the tomb.

Through the following nights she hears the howl and cry of her own heart, like that of an animal caught in a trap. She sees rabbits grazing in the garden under the moon.

One morning, many days later, Isabelle hears a peculiar low moan rising from under the house, drags open the heavy door and is met by a frenzy of flies.

The dog lies on her side, her paws crossed. Isabelle can see where she has worn a deep hollow in the dirt scattered with lizard bones and beetle wings. She kneels down beside her. The eyes of the dog are clouded with the terrible neglect. There is blood on her claws.

Thunder rolls in from the south. Rabbits dance on the grass as she lifts the dog and carries her up inside the house, and places her on the rug before the hearth. She holds warm milk and raw egg to her mouth, feeds her gently, and warms her before the fire. When the dog begins to lift her head a little, Isabelle's weeping falls from her like a curtain.

She runs up the stairs to the bedroom and drags Philippe's clothes from the drawer onto the floor, digging into jumpers, releasing the muffled smell of him into the air. She finds the revolver she had hidden from herself there. The heavy box of bullets.

She dials the number of Philippe's agent and a smoky voice answers.

Wordsmith Literary Agency.

It's Isabelle. I don't have a lot of time. I've seen Philippe on television. Is he back in Australia?

Yes, he's here for the launch of the new book.

Where?

The Capricorn bookshop tomorrow evening.

What time?

Eight.

The literary agent hesitates.

You...?

But Isabelle has already hung up.

~

Isabelle kneels down to light the fire. She struggles outside, only to find that the wood is wet. The wind cuts short the moan of the pines. Shivering, she reaches for a book and places it in the grate carefully. She sets a match to it and the pages catch. She takes her photographs of Philippe and some of his novels and feeds them to the fire. She holds out her hands to the flame and his words warm her.

With the next match she strikes a deal. She is sweating by the time she has collected her passport, the Italian lire, the airline ticket for Rome she bought today, and some clothes. She places them in a small suitcase, sets it by the door and heaps all his remaining books on the fire. It eats them and spills onto the wooden floor.

A bibliocaust.

Isabelle steps outside with the dog. The windows blaze. A flock of white cockatoos rises suddenly into the sky. Words spark above the bonfire of the house, which groans and twists like a body burning, and cries to the drift of ash settling upon the hanging swamp.

I am the mad wife, Isabelle says to the house.

I give you to the air.

⌒

In the dark, the lights from the car slide along telephone wires like a train on its tracks. From the high, moving purple cloud of the mountains, Isabelle drives the hour's journey to the Capricorn bookshop, the dog panting softly beside her on the seat. The revolver is hidden in the glove box. She drives, passing trucks sleeping on the side of the road until, on the freeway, she pulls over and turns off the ignition. She takes out the revolver and slides in the bullets.

Isabelle imagines the future, the moon writing on his tombstone, the script made Arabic by a century of weather. The wind from the passing traffic rocks her. The headlights of the cars sweep her face white. A train slides past in the rain. She thinks the death of the author is eternally written here and now. In the multiplicity of writing she finds an antique map, places it on a table, unfurls it, furnishes it with a finality, allows it to spring back. She is carrying out a systematic exemption of meaning. The body writing lies in a hollow of dirt. The author is absent. He is gone. The novel ends when writing at last becomes possible. She takes a piece of yellow paper, writes: *The birth of the author...*

Isabelle is growing still and clear at the entrance to the bookshop, the dog by her side. It is night, with a moon in the sky. Down here the rain has cleared. She stands on the edge of the busiest street in the city, where the moon looks bigger than the traffic lights as it meets the eyes of those heading up the street.

There is the clatter of shoes on the wooden floors in the Capricorn bookshop. People stand behind bookshelves, allowing a space around the television cameras where the author stands. Waiters in black T-shirts and long, white aprons lift silver trays laden with drinks above the eager crowd.

Isabelle can hear the frothy buzz of conversation and flinches as champagne corks burst from bottles. Voices are rising to a crescendo above the loud din of traffic coming in from the street. People have arrived at the book launch straight from work. Ties are loose. The moment waits.

She notices the famous critic, an editor, Philippe's publisher, and senses the air of expectancy. The literary agent is at the back of the room, loitering behind a bookshelf, smoking and agitated. Isabelle's eye is caught by the piles of the new novel stacked on tables. The cover is repeated on the shelves across the room, on the reviews with triumphant headlines tacked up on the walls.

Unused to the city, the dog is excited by the excess of stimuli, the abundance of odours. Her eyes are glinting in the lights, her mouth grinning. With a criminal calm, Isabelle stands quite still at the door, the revolver in her pocket, the dog keeping close, still a little weak. There is something of the fox in the way she throws back her head to sniff the air, revealing the white underside of her throat.

Isabelle watches Philippe put his hand to his mouth, cough, hitch up his trousers. His hair is cut so differently, sharply. He has put on weight. The moustache is gone and his mouth is thin, vulnerable. He seems much shorter, more tentative. She watches him look anxiously about the room, then find what he is looking for. Isabelle follows his line of sight to the lecturer in Romance languages, wearing cream linen and talking to the television crew. She catches the look he sends her, locks on to it as deftly as if it were a baseball that sinks into her waiting glove. She moves to his side. Her hand brushes his wrist, then moves to adjust the gold chain about her neck. Bending her head to one side, she touches an earring and leans close to him, murmuring. He relaxes a little, raises an eyebrow and smiles.

The cameras swing on to Philippe and the lecturer in Romance languages, and now they are two figures close together, illuminated, held in a pool of light apart from the crowd. People jostle for a position where they can see. The publisher takes a gulp of champagne and runs her thumb over the piece of paper she grasps. There is a line of sweat forming now on Philippe's forehead.

As he holds a book in the air, a roaring cheer rises from the crowded room. He speaks. The dog presses against Isabelle's leg, lifts a paw, registering the sound of Philippe's voice, for which she has waited so long. She struggles against Isabelle's hand, tugs at her, glances up in surprise when she meets resistance.

Philippe holds up his glass, which catches, in its curve, the reflection of movement from the door. The dog is howling now, a high-pitched keening sound as she crashes through the legs of the literati, her ears straining forward. Isabelle sees the savageness of passion, of love, and holds her breath as the dog prepares to dive, embrace his face, eyes, the crooked nose. She sees the look of fear upon Philippe's face replaced by recognition. Philippe steps towards the dog. Isabelle lifts the revolver and with one shot alters his script, changes the direction of things in an instant. She feels the blood drain from her heart.

The author steps backwards. The book and the glass are jolted into the air until they reach the point where they will arc no higher. She sees them falling, and hears his head striking the floor with a sound like a rolled-up newspaper thrown from a passing car.

The howling dog at his head, the red swelling from the hole in his neck: this makes sense of the explosion of blood to those watching the terrible disclosure his throat makes, the blood running like red ink on paper struck by rain.

As she flees, Isabelle hears the strings of Borodin's *Nocturne*, and imagines his coffin swirling on the surface of the sea, dancing, waltzing like a rudderless boat before it goes under. She glances back. The agent reaches him first and draws the dog away, stroking her fur, soothing her yowling anguish. And the two of them are there for a moment, like a boulder in a stream, before the others flood in upon the dying author.

The hysterical crowd has noticed neither Isabelle's departure, nor the arrival of forgiveness.

The Concerto Inn

It is early morning in the valley of the scribbly gums. Smoke is still sifting in plumes through the white limbs of the trees as the lecturer in Romance languages stands before the smouldering house. Her crumpled linen shirt is flapping in the breeze. She is exhausted from the hospital, the police, and there are dark streaks of rage under her eyes. Dr Rose shivers in the Katoomba air, which is colder than in the city, even in summer. She moves towards the foundations of the house, still sheltered by the remains of a floor. Inside, beneath the blackened floorboards, she smells the stench of rotting literature, glimpses the shocking neglect of Thomas Bernhard, startled by mildew on his spine, sharing a box with Roland Barthes.

She enters and towards the back she notices a tin trunk, decorated with pressed metal dragons, lodged near a hollow of dirt, covered in dust and ash. Scattered around it are small skulls, tibias, fibulas, other osteal remnants embedded in the soil. On her knees in the bones, she opens the trunk. A sharp, foreign perfume strikes her. She finds it lined with soft blue silk and wooden compartments, oval boxes. One box covered in green cloth contains a smaller brass box full of blue and turquoise glass marbles, a swatch of black hair, a silver ring, a dozen pencils sharpened to perfect points, erasers.

She picks out ash jars, blossom jars and an empty Mateus bottle from a neatly stacked pile. There is an inscription on the label in indecipherable, faded ink. Like a Chinese box, there are smaller boxes within each other, one covered in black linen, another with little drawers of yellow painted wood. She touches a large casket of soft, reddish-brown wood overlain with slabs of ivory, carved in low relief and delicately stained. Inside it she notices wads of paper. There are diaries, files, manuscripts, cards, notes, newspaper clippings, old proofs, contracts, photographs, magazines, faxes and letters: a whole literary life here. A photograph of two women, obviously sisters, slips from the pile. She examines it closely and realises that one of them is Isabelle. As she slips the photograph into her pocket, she recognises Philippe's script on a protruding piece of paper, and draws out the manuscript of his unfinished novel. The pages are a little ragged. She runs her hand quickly over the title, *The Concerto Inn*. As she had hoped, the sacked tomb of the house has yielded to her all its secrets: the message from Philippe's past has safely reached her.

The lecturer in Romance languages emerges from the dimness as the cannibal biographer, dazed with the success of what she has seen, and what she holds in her hand. She lets go of the breath she has been holding, and takes the papers back up to the warm car. Settling into the driver's seat, she begins to read Philippe's story.

Song to the moon

Italy.

There is a lamp in that name. A port of entry to another territory. Changing hemispheres has the allure of the fresh page. On the plane, Isabelle sleeps as if on bales of Chinese silk. Over Istanbul she is woken in the night by voices, or perhaps seagulls spinning trails across the Marmara Sea, and she hears a morning cry rise from the dark. She imagines her flight over green hillsides with tiny roofs surrounded by cypress trees, and the side of a cliff falling down to the sea. There is a village with a small tower. In early spring she journeys from the jade gate of Hong Kong to the stone tower of Italy, with the Escher etching her only map.

In Istanbul Isabelle stands behind a man who was stopped by the airport security guards, and forced to tip knives and forks from his pockets. There she spends a day in light drizzle that falls upon the Blue Mosque near the Hotel Sokullapasa. She seeks shelter in the Grand Bazaar, drinks apple tea and is dusted by green powder in the Spice Bazaar when she leans over to look at the Turkish delight. A young man hurries from behind the counter and brushes down her coat with a small broom.

The next day finds Isabelle walking from the Termini to the Hotel Positano, past black men whose shining faces are mirrors to Rome. Few people notice her. She is like a travelling hermit, encased within the envelope of her own plan.

The window in her hotel room opens onto a wall. There is a loud voice at the desk, talking on the phone. She hears a voice outside her door: I need towels. The light doesn't work. I have just come from Spain, and it is much better, cheaper. Are you sure this is the price?

In the morning the shower floods her room and she wipes the floor with a white towel. She catches the train. The fields between Rome and Florence are a soft green flecked with patches of yellow flowers.

In Florence the sky clears above Giotto's belltower as Isabelle makes her way to the Hotel Cristina on the via Condotta, a tiny street near the Duomo. She climbs a long, narrow staircase and is greeted by a man in a yellow shirt and a grey vest. He hands her a large key on a piece of string.

When Isabelle is woken early the next morning by the street-cleaning machine, she walks towards the sun rising over the Arno. She crosses the Ponte Vecchio, past wood once soaked in pigs' blood and now brushed with gold.

She drinks *camomilla* tea at the Caffè Concerto Paszkowski in the Piazza della Repubblica. A man opposite her, with a face like one of the Medicis, speaks to an invisible companion in soft Italian. His hair curls darkly about his face and he wears a long, grey woollen overcoat and black leather shoes that have been highly polished. He moves his hands in circles, listens to the other, laughs appreciatively while drinking a large Coke with a slice of lemon in it. Nearby is a woman whose mouth and nose fill up her whole laughing face. She sits in the sun with a man in a blue shirt.

That colour, thinks Isabelle, is the blue of a Fra Lippi robe. And it is this blue with which she is carefully composing her final journey.

⌁

Isabelle lingers in Florence long enough to learn the shape of the city. She secures a room for the night in an old convent in Fiesole. As she opens the door to her room, a breeze lifts the white netting, and taps the window against its casement. Far below, the Duomo floats in the pastel green haze that is Florence in the late afternoon.

In the Museo Bandini a wash of red paint is laid over the gold in Lotto's *Annunciation*. Everywhere in Italy Isabelle studies the faces in the annunciations, sees the message repeatedly delivered by an insistent angel. She is startled by the loudspeaker that breaks the silence and, in four different languages, commands her to move away from the pictures. She jumps back and leaves too quickly. From a public phone box she calls Madeleine in Paris. Isabelle's own annunciation of what she has done.

That evening, in her room in the convent above Florence, the dusk turns blue. After the light leaves the buildings along the Arno, she lies below the crucifix on the narrow bed, sleepless until the grey dawn. Her bones feel old, like those caught as relics, surrounded by gold in the Duomo. The perpetual catching after the mortal. Keeping it for as long as possible before it crumbles, cracks like honeycomb.

In Italy, Isabelle is seeking the balm of colour and light to draw out the poison within her, to be soothed by the voices of strangers in *pensiones*, the moving pictures outside the window of a train, the different texture of the food she eats. Craving the unfamiliar, she will journey with these things easing her, and allow Italy to gently insist its shape upon her.

In the dark chapel, the painting is the light. The frescoes are green. There is the procession of the three kings: the Medicis are entering Florence, striding past the hills of Fiesole. They are blessed, these people in their red stockings: Cosimo, Lorenzo and Giuliano. The robe of the emperor has red and gold for the sleeves, green and gold for the tunic. There is a leopard on a leash, a caravan of oriental and Italian merchants swaying through the Tuscan countryside. Gozzoli has mixed animal blood with alum for the Prussian blue, and glazed it with egg tempera. Transparent verdigris, gilded tin, all obscured by years of candle smoke. This colour enters Isabelle's skin and penetrates her cells.

A flock of young men and women appears near the Baptistery. They kiss. They laugh. Then, all at once, they fly off in different directions, their jackets and skirts like spreading wings. As they disappear past the statue of Brunelleschi, a white object falls from a coat to the ground. Wanting to capture some of their happiness, Isabelle wanders over to see what it is, and picks up a packet of small cigars. She places the cigars in her pocket. And as she thinks of her own journey ahead, her lungs burst with the colour of Italy, and there is a sudden sharp departure from the ruminations of her mind.

⌒

On the train to Venice, Isabelle falls asleep with her finger on a line in an open book. She takes with her into sleep the memory of this journey, and fragments of the passengers on the train, the villages she has rushed through, the houses along the track. Outside, through the blue, flat haze, lights appear in the early evening. The train passes a ploughed field, a roof of patched tiles, and crosses a bridge. Isabelle speaks softly the names of each of the places they pass through: like commas in a sentence, the painted cities of Italy.

Rain begins falling like hair combed down over the back of the sky. It spins across the window of the train. A man throws his coat over a little boy's head and shoulders as they cross a village street. A Japanese couple. Her skin of colourless glass. As he cracks his knuckles he leans towards the woman to say things that make her laugh. These things are navigational aids on Isabelle's journey.

Out the window, dark cypresses are set far apart upon the deep green fields. As the train slides around them, they move towards and away from each other in a spatial concerto, like figures in a piazza.

Beside her, on the seat, is the small rectangular suitcase on wheels; inside it, an alarm clock, some clothes. She wears Philippe's boots. In her lap there is a black cotton hat from Katoomba in which she has wrapped her bread, cheese, walnuts and wine. When a man in a field looks up at the passing train, his eyes absently attach to hers.

Isabelle keeps her ticket ready at all times and now she unwinds it as the conductor sways towards her. There are many stamps on the ticket, many different scripts, because she has been moving like this for weeks. She drifts across Italy as if in a balloon, free of direction. Crisscrossing the country, never staying longer than a few days in any one place.

They speed past birch trees in a field, smoke rising in front of a villa surrounded by white prunus. A dog stands on the roof of a house in a village. A drift of dark birds settles on water.

⌒

Upon her arrival in Venice, Isabelle takes the *vaporetto* from the station and rests upon the crest of water, the ebb and flow of her passage along the Grand Canal brimming with watercraft. The sun comes out and warms her, and the city reveals itself. Lustrous and iridescent, Venice absorbs, refracts and reflects light like the crystalline nacre of the pearl: something precious to be carried into the next world. Lapis lazuli from the Orient. She holds her face to the light and air, the barcarolle of the gull from the sea, the smell of salt and fish, the sound of the water lapping at wooden landing stages. Inside the mullioned windows of *palazzi*, she glimpses small *putti*, tapestries and brocades lit by lamps, frescoed salons. A decayed boat lies tethered at a mooring pole. A passing funeral boat is laden with plumes and flowers. At the end of this journey there is the golden orb of the Dogana da Mar floating in fine rain.

The room in the Al Gambero Pensione is dry and warm, with smooth white sheets. In the morning when she wakes, the light has already come and she feels like one of Fra Angelica's pastel angels.

⌒

Isabelle journeys south again, intent upon her purpose.

From the window of the train she greets the advancing warm colours, watches Naples, the fire city, sinking in sun, and writes in her notebook, upon her knees.

She finds the Ostello Mergellina behind the dark station, away from the noise of Vespas and cars. There is a room of her own for a night, possibly longer, so she leaves her things and takes a bus to Spaccanopoli. The bus passes a nun in falling folds of white cloth, watering geraniums in pots, and travels through cramped, dark streets with palm trees here and there. At Spaccanopoli she walks down to via Benedetto Croce, past tiny shops selling coral pendants, religious medallions and rosary beads. She wanders far into the narrow back streets where washing hangs from windows, high up on poles, like flags, and curses fill the air from time to time. A woman with black hands sits and smokes in the evening.

Inside a hall of quiet statues in dusky light, there are a mummified heart and a picture of a woman tortured by her husband, looking like a mermaid with her skirt tied at the bottom of her feet. She is naked from the waist up. Her eyes meet Isabelle's. Detached.

Isabelle sits in the courtyard and contemplates the next part of her journey. In the morning she will take the Circumvesuviana—past Vesuvius, which sent beings abruptly into their afterlives—to Sorrento. Then the bus to Amalfi.

For lunch she had eaten a sandwich on the train. This evening there is green pea soup at the Ristorante Giglio in the via Toledo. The regulars come in and settle at their tables. She takes the table of a man who finds himself obliged to turn quickly in circles while putting on his coat to leave. At the door, an umbrella is like a bunch of furled flowers in his hand.

Isabelle watches all of this as though it were a painting on a wall.

⌒

From blue mountains to blue grotto.

Having seen Naples, Isabelle walks along the white-walled laneways of Capri to the garden of Augustus. The museum of birds, yellow frescoes, hens in the monastery. From here the Faraglioni rise like stone sisters from the sea. She stays one night at the Hotel Maresca carved deep in the side of the hill above the Marina Grande. On its balcony she looks up from her notebook to see that the light has almost left the Amalfi Coast. Naples fades into the sea, which is completely still except where a small boat, far off, curdles the water.

Now, she thinks, I am closer.

The next day finds her on a blue Sita bus. With poise and grace a seagull glides above the bus as it swings over the edge of the Amalfi Coast. The corniche road is a line that disappears and returns on the southern side of the Sorrento peninsula, where the cliffs fall straight into the sea. She sees white cockatoos in a cage.

She reaches Amalfi, set in a broad cleft in the cliffs, white-painted houses built into its terraces. Here Isabelle changes to the smaller yellow bus for the climb up to the solid rock above the Valle del Dragone that is Ravello, where she will be nearer to the sky.

Yellow wattle flowers appear along the slopes through rough trellises made from tree limbs. She holds tightly as the bus negotiates the switchbacks. The road repeats itself and the bus announces its arrival at each corner with a sharp blast of the horn, swaying in and out of the sunlight so that Isabelle is almost lulled into sleep.

There is a blind girl on the bus, her head bent low. Suddenly she sets alight a piece of paper and, with a laugh, throws it out the window as the bus pauses at Scala and they are overtaken by a dark blue car with a white roof and a red stripe on the side. It is full of Caribinari. As Isabelle moves away from the window, the bus crosses the gorge to Ravello, from where she hears a dog's bark, reaching across from Scala. Isabelle leaves the bus and walks in the sharp air through a tunnel to the Piazza Vescovado, then along via Cimbrone, following the Ravello ridge where the Arabian-Sicilian buildings sit in silent, luxuriant gardens. She passes along stone walls with birds and violets emerging from cracks, until she comes to heavy wooden doors and pushes them open. She finds herself in the garden of the Villa Cimbrone. A curving, sandy path leads her through a lawn scattered with white flowers. There are flax, date palms, plane trees, *Cedrus atlantica* 'Glauca', early blossoming apple and cherry trees. She can hear the hooting cries of the bus as it makes its way back down to Amalfi.

When she comes to the end of the path, Isabelle is blinded by blue light. The Terrazza dell'Infinito hangs out over the cliffs, high above the water, edged by a line of stone heads, each concentrating its gaze out to sea. A short leap to the hereafter. She takes in the whole bay in one breath as a woolly white cat rolls in the sunlight, warming itself against a wall. Isabelle places herself carefully in Ravello, the way she would a piece on a chessboard, holding it with the tips of her fingers so as not to dislodge her other pieces.

Above the sea, she rings a bell at the gate of the white Villa Francescatti with its blue door. When she is admitted she takes a room for a night or two on the piano nobile. It's like a monk's cell, with a narrow bed, a stone floor, a mirror, a desk and chair. The light looks in through a deep window that gives a view out to the blue and white boats on the Gulf of Salerno. It allows the gaze out and in, partitions the interior and exterior space. There are little steps up to the window and the wooden shutters have its shape. On a round polished table sits a blue jug. The yellow tulips in the jug shine upon the wood. Placing her things on the bed, she takes her skin off with her boots, reads her own face in the mirror, and sits there for a time smoking a cigar. At the moment Isabelle ends her month's journey, she hears, moving amid seagulls' cries, the voice of a bell.

A few days after arriving in Ravello, Isabelle makes her way down to Amalfi, along the sea, where the heavy breast of water rests upon the shore. Silver fish are lying in the shadows of the streets, ready for the market. Isabelle climbs the wide, steep flight of steps up into the Duomo at the top of the piazza. She takes a white candle and holds it close to a burning one, dipping it until it flares a little and the flame grows brighter.

Outside, in the garden of the Chiostro del Paradiso, she looks up as bells begin to ring, right above her, moving and singing in the garden.

The museum holds an eighteenth-century sedan chair from Macau and, as she reaches out towards it, she feels a little faint and sits for a moment on the steps, beside a terracotta pot of red geraniums.

She has not eaten. Perhaps the Stendhal syndrome she has read about is affecting her and she is being overwhelmed by beauty: a common cause of treatment at the Santa Maria Nuova

Hospital in Florence. The syndrome was named because of the sensations Stendhal experienced after visiting the tombs of Michelangelo, Galileo and Machiavelli in Santa Croce.

The workmen restoring the Duomo clatter past Isabelle, down the steps to a cafe below. She follows them into the Caffè Pompeii, where she hears many voices, much movement. In the corner a fish pond is surrounded by pots of brightly coloured pelargoniums. Boxes, tins of cakes and chocolates are arranged on the shelves: mosaics of colour. A woman with thin legs is wiping all the boxes carefully with a damp cloth. She then takes up a vase and arranges olive leaves in a way that reveals their green faces, their silver backs. She places the vase on a black piano. A waiter is setting down spoons, taking up forks, removing white linen tablecloths and slipping them into drawers at the foot of a cabinet packed with bottles of red wine, biscuits, blue and silver packages of chocolates. There are all different kinds of pasta in dusky, earthy colours: tagliatelli, fisarmoniche, fusilli buco, legumata, bocche di lupo and conchiglie. Isabelle reads the labels of the packages as though they were the titles of books.

She seats herself outside at a table set on large, dark grey flagstones at the edge of the piazza. There are throngs of people around, their voices rising and rising like waves. A woman calls down from a window above the piazza. Everything is close. Isabelle can hear the breathing, the smiling, of people, and within her is ringing her own response to the bells she'd heard a few moments before. The spring sun presses her against the white pillar at her back. A butterfly folds the air. She takes out a cigar to smoke.

Buon giorno. My name is Paolo, says a waiter with a thick grey moustache. You have come from far? You can rest here. What would you like? I have pasta. I have *vino.*

A little bow.

He calls to a small girl who is sitting at a nearby table, coloured pencils spread before an open, blank page. Bia, bring bread for the lady.

Isabelle concentrates on Paolo's pasta, and the fresh bread. A timid black dog appears on the steps of the Duomo, its paw folded like a deer's. There is sleep or infection in its eyes, and small tracks of blood from an injured paw.

A man in a green shirt and olive trousers sits in the corner by the steps, reading a newspaper. His hair is grey against smooth brown skin. He looks up over the top of his glasses and, noticing the dog, bends down to pat it. Isabelle takes out her notebook and writes sideways, a hand over the page, alert to the possibility of an interruption. When she turns a page, she runs her hand over the fresh one like a blind woman, as though she is feeling for what there is to come.

She senses the man looking at her large, ill-fitting boots, the black coat hanging over the chair beside her. He seems to be studying her and turns his head to read the foreign label on her boots: *5 Percy St, Prospect, Sth Australia*. Isabelle folds them under the chair and writes on, with the afternoon sun making stained glass of her wine.

The little girl approaches the man.

Luca, do you want to see me pull my Band-Aid off?

No.

I'm going to pull my Band-Aid off.

No, Bia.

She pulls the Band-Aid off to reveal a woundless knee. Nothing. She laughs at Luca, who reaches down and offers the dog some gnocchi. He takes out some pink paper and shows Bia how to do origami.

An Englishman comes in and pats Bia on the head. His name is Kevin, Paolo tells her, but to Bia, who is unable to pronounce the *K*, he is Heaven.

~

Isabelle finds herself arranging to extend her stay at the Villa Francescatti. Each evening she travels by bus down from Ravello to the Caffè Pompeii, just as the last light of day is falling down the Duomo steps. Paolo greets her. Luca is always there before her. He doesn't look up until she is seated, then nods and returns to his paper. Paolo brings him pasta.

One puttanesca, sings Paolo to Luca to the tune of 'Guantanamera'.

One puttanesca, sings Luca to Paolo.

One puttan–e–s–c–a, they both sing.

Paolo sits down with Isabelle when things are a little slower and, gesturing to the kitchen, says, Sorcha, she cooks like a dream. She is Irish. I met her on the island of Ischia, where we were on holidays when we were both young. We wrote letters to each other for years. We married in Naples.

He smoothes the white tablecloth.

My father was injured in Bologna in 1941 and spent three weeks in hospital in Naples. They sent him to the Hotel Excelsior Vittoria in Sorrento for a week to recover and he went back for his honeymoon. So we did, too. Sorcha said the choice was difficult: either a week in Blackpool wearing kiss-me-quick hats and eating fairy floss and fish and chips, or a week in Sorrento at the Excelsior Vittoria.

He draws back a moment, his hands in the air, palms upward. Then he smiles suddenly: She thinks we made the right choice!

He winces a little. A car in Florence hit Sorcha but we went to Sorrento anyway, after she got out of the hospital. There were many important guests. A neurosurgeon from Osaka, an engraver from Sussex. And us. It was winter. We had a double room that looked over the Bay of Naples. On the first night there were thunder and lightning and much rain. We spent our days sitting looking out over the sea, watching Vesuvius come and go in the mist. When Sorcha could walk a little we wandered in the orange grove. You had to avoid the falling oranges.

He shapes his hands into a bowl.

Then it cleared and we took the bus to Amalfi and it was then that we decided to make it our home.

Bia interrupts her father to give Isabelle a plaster hippopotamus painted silver, with a pink tongue, and a miniature cactus for her room in Ravello.

When she was young, Sorcha was a teacher in a small village near Dublin, he says. But here the schoolchildren are uncontrollable, so she gave it up after a year.

He picks up a fork and sets it down again.

She believes all Italians get too excited at the slightest excuse.

Isabelle can see that Sorcha is faded now, and tired of having her belongings snatched from her in the streets of Naples. She can see that Bia carries the light her mother had as a girl.

Paolo points to the portrait on the wall of Bia that Luca has painted. Her bearing is proud. He has caught in her face the chiaroscuro of renaissance painting that rises from ochre, charcoal and sinopia. She sits in silk adorned with the Chinese patterns that came to Italy along the Silk Road. Behind her, a luminous rendering of the landscape: the sky of crushed lapis lazuli, hyacinths on yellow silk, elegant architectural settings. In the chromatic brilliance there is the stillness of Bia, the extreme beauty of her hands.

~

One evening Luca sits outside beside Isabelle. He unfolds a large sheet of thick paper covered in intricate drawings, and smoothes it out across the table. He pours a glass of amber wine and they eat small wild strawberries and oranges. His hand taps her arm as he tells her of the architect who is drawing up the plans for his house in Ravello. He speaks to her with the tongue of music, the wash of oratorio. He smiles at her and carefully peels a ribbon of orange rind that comes to rest and lies across the plate. He considers her seriously.

You are like a woman who has survived a war, or a terrible illness: a transparent construction. I have noticed that you have a particular knowledge and a particular vulnerability. A car crash? In any case, something violent and cruel.

A flush of pigeons sweeps the piazza. In the blue of his shirt, Luca is like a fish caught for a moment in Murano glass. But it is the way he treats Paolo, Bia and the dog that she notices as much as the colour of skin, eyes. As an idea, a presence, he was forming within her gradually, almost imperceptibly, like a wave swelling in the sea.

I'm so glad you've come, he says. I'm exhausted here. Paolo talks until there are holes in your stomach.

Luca is exotic to Isabelle. He comes from a family of artists. When he speaks of them in the Caffè Pompeii, she thinks that the names of his friends, his family, are like the names of medieval cities on an antique map, spread out upon the table in an ordinary room. She journeys to them, learns a few words of the language, spins the currency in her palm, and then catches the train to the next place. This time it's Luca. He's a small walled city, with a river running along the line of the sun. She knows the journey will continue through the country that is his family, and end in the house that is his heart.

⌒

Isabelle stands before Luca at the door to her little room. Her eyes are glazed by light. She feels poised like a swimmer above the pool.

You remind me of one of Giacometti's tall figures, he says. The ones he finally produced after obsessively creating and destroying tiny ones during the war years. They became, very gradually, larger, sparer. There is a particular unapproachable, remote woman, standing with her hands at her side, with something passive but indestructible in the rough surface.

Isabelle makes him tea, moving quietly like a monk about her task, concentrating on the pot, the cups. She places the tea things before him. The cups rattle a little. The tea spills. As she sets a cake upon his plate, she feels his eyes upon her like columns of the clear, blue smoke of burning ambergris.

He tells her about the reconstruction of his house: the sanded poplar, linden wood. The fresh, fast frescoes on the southern wall. She can hear the colours sing as he speaks of miniver brushes, gesso. The house, which sits in the most beautiful garden in Ravello, has been growing like a living thing with muscles, bones, he says.

She settles, sits quietly with him at the table and turns her head to the high window of her room. Placing her hand on the wooden chair frame, the raking light falling across her fingers, she strokes the wood as though it is a piece of silk floating in the window. Her fingers move to her lips as she imagines herself standing in Luca's garden. She feels like a stream of light from head to shoulder: a fall, a fold, a wavy line.

Now her hands lie folded in her lap, fingers curled, the silk of skin passive, and he seems to wait for her to raise her hand, to lean forward and set it gently on the back of his neck, between hair and collar. The touch of the bow upon the cello.

As he is leaving he places a small gift in her hand without a word. It's a silk sack as blue as Chagall's air, like the ones in the gold cabinet in Naples that contained the remains of nuns, each labelled with her name. Inside is a little intaglio he has carved out of a peach-stone—a brooch. She sees that it is an eye, the centre of which has been hollowed out and filled with minute, clear stones. He pins it on her black coat.

I need to keep an eye on you.

⌒

Luca takes Isabelle to his house on via San Francesco.

Halfway down the walled lane, a lavender and orange numbered tile announces the entrance, concealed by foliage. A frescoed loggia receives them and behind it is a dark, ancient building. Isabelle lifts her eyes to the new curved roof above the stone.

There are yolks in the mortar to make it strong, he tells her.

Below the villa, a hanging garden falls down the side of the valley. The garden unveils the view gradually as he leads her through the pleached alleys of the *cedrario*—the orange grove—to the pond, full of koi. Some of the fish have dark, rich red fins and cheeks, while others are golden yellow, floating amid water hyacinth. Small beccaficos fly up as they approach the birdbath, the water shivering and dimpling as they plunge their small bodies into it. The air is filled with the buzzing of their wings as they hover above the water, drying their feathers. Butterflies feed on nectar. Here, he tells her, the Rosaflora camellia flowers will fall upturned, landing like cats.

They pause a moment, by the gate, and he turns to her. Suddenly his telephone calls him away. Isabelle stands quite still, resting in the dreamscape of the garden, floating in blue air until he returns a minute later. They enter the villa and there is more glass, a gathering of light and coloured plaster walls, bare wooden floors covered with rugs. Like a good story, it seems that nothing might be added, taken away or altered, but for the worse. Above them a small stone tower looks to Capri and Naples, and at the front of the villa is a glass room with four chimney pots on the roof.

He leads her to a room of egg-yolk yellow where his paintbrushes hang in a row, each a different thickness. The room is full of the watery transparency of Venetian *cristallo*, an engraved potash-lime glass, wooden sculptures, spiral shells in bottles, lemons, photographs, cushions, jugs of flowers with petals the shape of Byzantine windows, round stones, fine pots, blue plates, dried gardenia flowers in vases of opaque white glass, a pear in a bottle.

On a ledge at the window, two doves that had been sitting together like votive hands rise into the air as they approach. Isabelle leans out the window and looks down to the portico, the arch of which has the line of a long neck. From above, the koi and the flowers in the garden look like a Japanese wedding party gathering on the lawn.

Like a red tulip, life is growing in Isabelle's breast again.

Luca uses language to touch her.

Come out on the Gulf of Salerno. I'll bring the boat. You bring the tea, he says one evening when he walks towards her through a door, a wave of warmth entering before him like the swell of sea before the bow of a boat. It is as though they are walking through the laneways of Capri and suddenly glimpse, in the eyes of the other, the turquoise sea, the Faraglioni.

The wood of the boat speaks of the time of night to the gentle water sliding there. They glide, in deep dark, to the shore of sea from the shore of land, and settle in the crevice of a wave. They wait for the moon. When it comes, in the phosphorescent sheen of its light, Isabelle becomes visible to herself as she extends her hand to the white teapot and makes rose tea. She unwraps aromatic almond biscuits as he sips his tea. There is no other place now—just this boat on this sea. In the mirrored night there is only the sound of oars dipping into the luminous water. The lights from Positano flash like foxes' eyes and guide them back to shore.

A week later in the house in Ravello, Luca is sitting on a stool with a wooden figure resting against his body. The bloom is still visible on the wood. Isabelle sits nearby writing in her notebook. He raises his hand to his forehead and taps his fingers there. As he carves the wood, he is painting light in a burning space.

Smelling the soft perfume of camphor laurel, Isabelle looks up from her book and watches him work. His ideas seem to her to grow from the wood as he whittles away until there's almost nothing remaining. The wood appears weightless against the blue plaster walls, possessing great lightness in form. He takes his Pfeil fishtail chisel and curves it into the hollow, deepening, lessening with each movement, swaying as he strokes its sharp edges away, the surfaces swelling and subsiding like flesh. The thing with wood is that you have to cut across the grain, not down it, otherwise it splits, he says.

Beside the window, which at once gives a view and is a view of itself, the folds in his standing sculpture repeat the grain in the Amalfi Coast as it catches the late afternoon light. In the centre of the sculpture there is a space, the absence there having as much meaning as a solid presence. In its upward movement there is the camphor laurel tree from the dark forests of China and pieces of sandalwood dropping in the forest like rain, as men long ago went into the hills in clothes made from tree bark. They took sago to eat, and gathered camphor, which formed crystals and was called plum flower camphor. They collected broken bits, which they named rice camphor.

As his sculptures die with the light, he feeds her white Italian chocolate.

One piece for every month you are in Italy, he tells her.

Isabelle laughs. But there are hundreds of pieces here!

His lips carve a smile.

⌒

One evening Paolo plays 'Night and Day', puts the ashtray to his ear and dances across the floor. Excitedly, Bia's fingers fold back her hair. She claps her hands, takes the paws of the dancing dog and whirls about the room. In the polished mirrors of the Caffè

Pompeii, Isabelle and Luca see themselves reflected a thousand times.

A woman in a black dress begins to dance. Another, older woman in a long, green silk jacket becomes her partner and dances with a face as still as stone, her eyes downcast.

Luca leans over to Isabelle. Her name is Rose, he says. But she can't pronounce her own name. It is the *R* that trips her up. So when she answers her phone she says, 'Guess who this is.'

A woman called Francesca comes in and greets them. A student of Luca's, she is sixty, very large, a little deaf, and spent many years in prison in Naples. She visits him in Ravello each week for her drawing lesson. Once she made his name out of old typewriter keys attached to a silver pin. He says she has artist's hands, as deft as a blind harpist's. For her ink paintings, Luca has taught Francesca to use handmade paper that has been hung out to dry like laundry. This gives it a fine grain so that it absorbs the ink without bleeding.

The paper must be in love with the ink, he said. They have to marry.

Francesca's face has the same grain as her hair. She wears dirty sneakers with coloured wool for shoelaces and carries a plastic shopping bag. She sits at her usual table, exhausted for a moment, like a coat thrown absently across the back of a chair. She takes out a diet book called *Whipped Cream and Martinis* and reads it like a novel. As she drinks coffee and smokes, she draws in an exercise book in black ink, oblivious to the music, the dancing. A man who has been drinking beer through a straw, and has heard from others that she is an artist, approaches her. He bows and shakes her hand, which is impatient and longs for the pen.

An oak and silk chair, blue in the evening light, stands with its rectangles and squares and the polished curves of wood in between, the bars of its back leaning into the shadows of the room. The round glasses illuminate Luca's face.

They move about in the dusk like two moths blinking their wings, drifting toward the light that each is. The air is sodden with the scent of bergamot orange blossom. His body is a wave upon hers, his breath the soughing and sighing of sea. Isabelle falls deeper and deeper, smells the clean, warm salt smell of his limbs enfolding her, feels the long line of his body displacing her in space.

It's only the moment we hold, she murmurs. The orange blossom's heavy cloak of perfume is loosened in the night. As she diminishes, her voice grows stronger. She finds the sweet dip into shadow of his throat. Her head presses into his arms, the curve of spine delicately cupped. Form reflecting form. They breathe each other out and in. His hands find the slope of her breast, and a deep current moves within her as he traces constellations across her skin, embroidering her flanks with his touch. A shiver follows along her bones. Her lips part and she tastes the saltiness of skin. In this deeply realised moment, she divulges herself to him.

In the second before she closes her eyes, Isabelle hears the song of Luca's voice, and the past moves aside to let the present in.

~

They sleep.

In the night she wakes, thinking there are voices, but they are seabirds calling in the dark. She sighs. I dreamed I had long hair. I was dying of thirst in the desert. I drank my hair.

His breath is upon her, breaking in the lung of the sea.

They sleep. And Isabelle is lost somewhere in the geography of his arms. Folded in upon herself like a swan, she draws closer into the shelter his body makes.

In the morning there is the soft bumping of the shutter in the breeze. She wakes, drawn into consciousness by the pure song of a bird. The window is imbued with light. She opens the glass and looks down into the garden. A bird, carrying the light of dawn upon its breast, passes above her.

When Luca wakes they swim down in the sea, where stones lie like eyes beneath the green, filmy water. In the lilac air above them, a curtain waves at a window and the dog tries to fly after the seagulls near the shore.

As they walk barefoot to the water, the heat makes Isabelle think of the smell rising from dry gum leaves in the bush, struck by sun. She remembers how cold the sea was in Tarwin, no matter what the season. She remembers being at the Prom with her parents and that French teacher of whom they had all become so fond. There was a turning point: Isabelle was present for it but she never understood its significance. There was a disquiet in Madeleine that had its origins in that day, and which isolated her from everyone. Isabelle recalled the French teacher's cry of pleasure as she picked up what turned out to be a little seahorse encrusted with sand. And then Madeleine rushing in a rage into the icy water.

Now Isabelle's skin gleams as she draws herself into the sun from the sea. The air receives her like a breath.

An auburn-haired woman, suddenly alarmed for some reason, cries out urgently to her child: Vittorio, Vittorio, you come away from the sea.

⌒

With the passage of time, Isabelle finds herself more and more often at the house in Ravello. The neighbours, full of noise, also come with their children. They bring Luca herbs and he gives them flowers from his garden. There is always music, and a radio blares if there is a soccer match on in Siena. Luca throws his hands in the air, hugs Isabelle when they score, swears when his team loses, and drops into the chair near the window. In the middle of the game he runs down the stone steps to ring a little bell to summon the koi in the pond for feeding, or to scatter pellets for the two one-eared rabbits he calls the Van Gogh Sisters. Isabelle thinks that Luca is like Albert Tucker, who said that he sought the golden thread in the day. There is an innate sense of loyalty about him, and generosity when she tells him about Madeleine.

Tell Madeleine to come. I'll make her *bucatini alla pineta*.

And there is the incantation of the recipe.

Bia asks him for his pencils as she sits at the kitchen table. She is making a small illuminated manuscript about the life of the dog and has written the narrative in horizontal bands, the figure of the dog set against a dark stripe of blue. Each page is decorated with scenes from the dog's new life, beginning with the day it appeared on the Duomo steps outside the Caffè Pompeii. She has designed intricate borders out of her initials. Near her elbow is the Venus flytrap that she gave Luca for his birthday. For weeks she had collected flies for it until he told her that it was becoming obese. Days later, while searching for his favourite pencil, he had found a little forgotten pile of dead flies in Bia's pencil case.

She tells Luca about her art teacher at school.

Oh, him, he says. I know him. He's about as interesting as a colourless koi. And ugly. Too ugly for fish food.

Bia and Isabelle giggle.

Luca breaks salt with a hammer. He feeds them ginger, garlic, broccoli, chicken, fruit, coconut gelato, blueberries, orange leopard marmalade. Though he loathes roses, he knows of Isabelle's fondness for them and presents her with a rosebush to plant in a part of the garden he now calls the *rosario*. He gives her fragile, yellow-toned paper that smells like honey, and teaches Isabelle and Bia to play 'Pass the Pigs'.

As if she is outside herself, Isabelle hears her own voice laughing like the tongues of bells throwing out music, until it's falling, falling like leaves about her.

One evening, Isabelle walks through the translucent azaleas in Luca's garden. Leaving the island of her day, she wades through poppies waving like seaweed on the floor of the sea. It has rained and the wet blooms sweep her past the looking-glass koi in the pond and on to his door with the soft, easy strokes of Amalfi blue. The door is sheltered by a tree with hard timber and deeply divided leaves, its trunk as smooth as the face of a mirror. She pauses a moment under the roof the lamplight gives her, and inhales the scent of cut box. She hears Bach's cello suites in the air and the anticipation of his presence is like the knowledge of the next note.

Does she sleep or wake?

Luca is the head on the Terrazza dell'Infinito, thrown back in the silver gelatin of night, high in the Ravello cold. She reaches for lips and finds tangled waves of hair, as grey as scribbly gums in the curled moon. The shadow of his head falls upon her face as he leans over her.

I have never lived in the house of love, she tells Luca. In Katoomba, I wasn't really there. I was like a woman waiting for the last days of Pompeii.

~

Some mornings, after waking in her room in Ravello, Isabelle walks through the lanes, catches the bus down to Amalfi to the Caffè Pompeii, and takes the table by the window. She places a small, white packet of sugar under one leg of the table to settle it. Paolo brings her tea at eight. She writes to Madeleine in the blue light.

Come to Ravello.

She can hear the sea, the movement of the Duomo bell. In the evenings here she sometimes plays 'Song to the Moon' on the piano. She finds that she no longer dreams of falling, has relaxed, and holds herself in a different way. She enters into the stream of things, discovering that the world is no longer unsafe.

Looking into the fish pond by her table, she sees reflections like thoughts, ideas, words swimming in the water. Some are muted in colour, some golden and waving slowly, or occasionally darting to the surface. When there's a ripple on the surface, one word becomes another, or one part of a word or idea is enlarged while another is diminished.

The talk rises as the morning goes on. Occasionally a couple of tourists come in. Isabelle realises that she no longer applies that word to herself. Luca, the blue air, the sweep of cobalt sea and sky are all working inside her with their needle and thread.

Francesca rushes into the cafe and sits beside Isabelle. She prods Isabelle's bag with her foot. I thought it was the dog you had under there.

She screams at Paolo to bring her coffee. She removes her false teeth and sands them with a nail file. She comes here to draw while Isabelle writes. Somehow Francesca knows that Isabelle's dreams are full of foreign places, a scattering of tongues, the sound of worms eating soil. Like her own.

Francesca tells Isabelle that in the prison in Naples she had drawn to the sounds of muffled crying coming from other cells, a quiet slicing of flesh. Drawing is her language of resistance.

Why were you in prison, Francesca?

I murdered my father. I stabbed him with a Staysharp knife.

<hr>

What are you writing, Bella? Luca asks, and she offers him the pages.

It's a story called 'Song to the Moon'.

He takes the pages and wanders away to read them, eating burnt toast. Later there is the smile that she knows from the blue light of dawn in his house. Her eyes meet his, and she lifts her head to receive his smile.

Bia reads it and scolds her. It was a silver rhinoceros I gave you, not a hippopotamus. I don't mind, though, if you just change it.

These are her first readers.

Isabelle cuts Luca's hair in the garden, and as it falls to the grass he plucks the old winter hair from the dog at his feet. She is talking to him about the concert they had listened to the evening before in the Rufolo gardens, planning a trip to Naples. They will take Bia with them. She is laughing now as Luca emerges newly shorn from her scissors. She notices there is some new part of her own voice that she has never heard before. It is odd to discover such a thing about myself, she thinks. That the person that I am, the voice that I have in the presence of one particular person, is so different from the voice that I had, the person that I was.

⌒

On her birthday, in May, Luca sets the round table out in the *giardino segreto* for lunch, while Isabelle strings red Japanese lanterns across the garden, each with a candle inside for Bia to light at dusk.

The sky is the colour of blue ink; there is a deep pink rose in the garden near the table. The petals fall onto the glass that the pond makes. Through a dark hollow in a corridor of old trees is a doorway of light, a window to the path scattered with rhododendron petals. The low branches of a tree lift in the gentle breeze, swaying like the heavy skirt of a priest crossing a street.

Isabelle wears a dress that Sorcha has made for her from soft rust and mauve silk. Luca gives Isabelle a brooch of dull, beaten gold, with a dash of cinnabar in the centre, and a wooden box in which to keep the small sculptures, the brooches, he gives her.

Isabelle covers the table with a white cloth and smoothes it with her hands. She sets places for Sorcha, Paolo, Bia and Francesca while Luca makes *passato di patate* for them. He melts yellow butter in a deep pot. He sautés the potatoes and leeks and stirs in vegetable broth, moving quickly and surely about the kitchen, his arm about Isabelle as she cuts the bread. He ladles the soup into six blue bowls. He places chives and toasted bread on the swimming surface, then prepares another plate.

In Australia, what do you call this—sparrow-grass?

Asparagus, she smiles as he pours *vermentino di sardegna* in a thin-walled glass. She shaves the straw-gold scaled *parmigiano*, which has been made from cows' milk in an enormous copper cauldron shaped like an upside-down bell. Now it lies in slivers on the plate.

After the main meal, they taste the sweet marsala, mascarpone and eggs of tiramisu as the old trees wave about them. Bia slips off into the shadows by the Irish strawberry tree, slowly revealing a smooth mahogany trunk beneath its jagged bark. The dog comes to lie under Luca's chair and the talk dies down in the warmth of the afternoon. He pours them a golden liqueur he has distilled in glass vessels from teardrop cumquats. Isabelle watches his hand falling again and again upon the dog's sleeping head.

With coffee, he gives them *amaretti*, *lingue di gatto*, and Isabelle thinks of the curl of the words from her pen.

⌒

Walking between them through the backstreets of Naples, past fish hanging gutted on strings in the sun, Bia takes Isabelle's hand, and Luca's. In the Piazza Dante, Isabelle buys a Polaroid camera, and Bia takes a photograph of them together.

In the evening, as the sun fades over the Bay of Naples, Bia races ahead of them to look at red ballet shoes in a window.

They wander through the narrow streets after her, leaning forward, their arms about each other lightly, looking into each other's faces as if looking into a lighted window or a doorway.

In a cafe in the Piazza Bellini, they drink coffee and eat balls of hard bread. A boy walks on the glass roof above them to retrieve a soccer ball. They watch a man across the street go into a shop with a tulip in his hand. He emerges a second or two later with a bottle in a paper bag. Isabelle thinks that she will bring Madeleine to such places when she comes. She draws out a piece of Japanese mulberry paper and an envelope she has bought. On the front she writes Madeleine's address in Paris. On the piece of paper, she writes *via San Francesco 2, Ravello*, and slips it inside.

As they sit there, Bia shows Isabelle the Polaroid. She and Luca are standing in the doorway of a rosy building. Luca is laughing at her. And Isabelle is standing beside him, as though gathering her body to launch herself joyfully into the air like a bird ready to fly out above the curving coast of the bay. It is an image of herself that Isabelle has never seen before. She looks at the photo as if it were of a stranger.

After Isabelle posts her letter, they drive home from Naples, past Vesuvius looming in the dark. The moon hangs in the rear window. Luca's cheekbones are lit by headlights. Bia sleeps, humped like a bony bird, between the dark shapes of Isabelle and Luca, lashes like dark feathers on her face, fingers in the curl of sleep.

The dog can't come, Bia had said when they planned the trip. It has flews.

Isabelle thinks of the Black Death. Of fleeing.

Flews.

On the car radio they listen to 'Staircase to the Stars', and drive on home in the night to where the little dog is tapping her nails.

Waiting.

⌒

In Luca's garden, petals swim like koi at the bottom of the pond, or drop like tiny hands upon his step.

It is a special soup that I am cooking today, he says as he heats olive oil in a deep pot and chops onions, celery and tomatoes. He pours cups and cups of boiling water over the vegetables and stirs in rosemary and salt. Isabelle carries the two blue bowls to the kitchen and slices the olive bread. She places a piece of bread in each bowl while Luca beats the eggs and then pours them over the bread. He ladles in the soup and grinds pepper. With it they eat potatoes like warm eggs.

At the end of this early summer's day, he will spend the evening carving a new piece of wood, releasing the fragrance of camphor laurel into the air. Isabelle will write the end of her story. In the soft dusk he will walk about the wood on the floor, and dream of the raw silk of her forehead, and the wild silk of her brow.

— Madeleine

A foreign country

I remember that my father was fond of quoting, *The past is a foreign country; they do things differently there.* And it was to both the past and my father that my thoughts immediately turned in that first moment of shock.

I caught sight of the photographs in a copy of *Le Monde* that had been discarded on the table in Le Fumoir, the cafe where I was drinking my coffee and gazing at the Louvre and the gardens of l'église St-Germain through the great windows. There was something about the shape of the background in the first photograph that caught my eye, that spoke to me of vestiges of the past. I flattened the newspaper on the table and examined the photographs more closely, my heart beating quickly, careful not to betray my agitation to those around me.

So, it's finally happened, I thought. The reckoning of time. For both of us, perhaps. Why else would there be Isabelle's face in the picture? They could have cropped her out. It seemed the time had come. After all these years of waiting for it. If it weren't for Xavier I could almost be relieved. There must surely be something akin to relief in being found out after such a long time?

In the photograph I am embalmed in the moment by the camera. I'm at Isabelle's wedding to Philippe. There is a dark smudge at the edge of the photograph and I remember my mother suddenly removing herself from it at the last minute, my father's disappointment, and her careful insistence. She didn't wait to see Isabelle and me hold ourselves to the camera, motionless for a moment, then dissolve into a movement towards our father, standing on the other side of the room, lowering the camera. So in the photograph in *Le Monde* I am looking directly at him, and now across the years I have become the object of my own gaze. The photograph reveals something of our fate, unknown to Isabelle at the time—as clear to me as the way bones are formed and hold themselves as a frame for a face.

As children Isabelle and I looked the same, and in the six months or so before I overtook her in height, people mistook us for twins. We each knew what the other was thinking without asking, and still do. I had never existed without her. We would sit together cross-legged, our backs against the wall, reading and eating honey from a jar on the floor, or watch fireballs roll across the paddock, sharing these things, like the times we spent with our father, the animals we kept. But she was much quieter than I, and had none of the affectations that I developed. I admired everything about Isabelle. Sometimes I believed that our thoughts were so much alike that we were one person. I could be speaking and become aware that I had Isabelle's voice and think: That's what Isabelle would say, that's the rise and fall of her voice, the exact tone of her expression. I wanted to be her so much and set about copying her handwriting carefully and making it my own style, even though it sloped backwards because she was left-handed.

As an adult I carried the thought that she blamed me. She left school and worked as a teacher in the city. Then she met Philippe and went to live in the Blue Mountains. At her wedding, our eyes met and we laughed at the irony of that: she married the Frenchman who was the brilliant young writer when I was the one obsessed with words and all things French. On the day of her wedding, after the photograph had been taken, I stood beside Isabelle, watching Philippe talking to the guests.

They say we do that, I said.

Do what?

Marry our fathers.

Far beyond us, out of the range of the photograph and the time, are the grey granite cliffs of the Prom, the quartz, pink and white felspar and black mica sparkling out over Bass Strait, which separates South Gippsland from Tasmania. Across the sky, slashes of dark cloud would appear. Further west, along the coast, was Cape Liptrap and, upon the dark sea, the white lighthouse that flashed three times every fifteen seconds to warn ships of the treachery that lay below the surface of the sea there. Some nights, across the paddocks, I could hear the surf screaming in Venus Bay.

Our place was called Tarwin, an Aboriginal word meaning *thirsty*. It lay three miles inland; three thousand acres of lush green pastures, rich peat soil; a river on two sides seeking the sea, and an artificial channel, with silver eels in it, running around the rest of the land, draining the swamp and leaving rich grazing land flush with strawberry clover for cattle.

The house had been built in the middle of this infinite, silent landscape, on the one slight rise in the land for miles around. It was arrived at by travelling along a clay road and passing through our gate and over an old, rattling white bridge.

It was protected from the west by oak trees, graceful in shape and proportion. My mother grew white irises in the black dirt. She told me that in ancient times the iris was believed to have meant: *I have a message for you.*

Inside the house were the perfumes of wood and roses, the aroma of cakes and biscuits lingering in the warmth in winter. The smell of polish was pervasive. There was a fireplace in every room, huge double-hung windows and double-beaded walls. Outside the windows were swathes of deep green. The stone at the hearth in the kitchen was sunken and worn smooth with a century of kneeling at the stove to fill it with wood from the old box. A jigsaw puzzle would sit on a low table in the kitchen near the stove for weeks on end, waiting for its last pieces to be matched up and clicked into place.

On the wall of the dining room, catching a little light from a casement window, hung a portrait of my family, painted by Mr Garbini, an Italian immigrant who sharefarmed a neighbouring property. My father gave Mr Garbini a photograph taken of the four of us together outside the church in Fish Creek, and he set to work immediately in a shed behind his farmhouse. I sometimes sat with him there while he painted. I watched him take a loaf of gesso and use his thick fingers and his palms to smooth it out over the canvas. He kept liquid colours in jars and stored them in a little chest. On top of the chest was a long box with a seal that contained leather sacks of ultramarine blue sent from Italy by a merchant who sold only blue. He said that the more you ground the colours, the more perfect the tint became. His charcoal was made from slowly roasting twigs he collected from the paddocks. They became slender coals for drawing the first sketch. He wouldn't allow me to watch him complete the painting and it wasn't until he hung it on our wall that I could see why.

The figure of my father seemed to provide the support for the rest of us. His features were ascetic, his face hollow and intense. Mr Garbini had caught my mother's melancholy in strong, sculptural contours. He had given Isabelle and me hands and features that carried some grace but did not dispute the fact that we had not been blessed with the beauty of our parents. Our clothes were depicted in a soft, deeply folded drapery style, in colours that were pure and clear in their intensity. In all our figures, a clarity of pose, expression, gesture.

The colour scheme of the interior of the house was muted, giving prominence to the four figures in the foreground in a calm dusk, with the light from one side and behind. A vase of bright, fleshy flowers stood on a table. The odd aspect to the portrait was the background. Through a wide window and an opening curtain was a clear, faraway landscape of azurite sky, sea, and a coastline remarkable for its fluency of line. He had positioned our figures and rendered our characters against this precisely observed, foreign landscape.

This is certainly an improvement, Garbini, my father laughed, indicating the brightly lit background, the odd-shaped tree.

That is the carruba tree of Ravello, said Mr Garbini. When you have been everywhere else, you go to Ravello.

⌒

When I was born, three years after Isabelle, it was our father who named me, as he had named Isabelle before me. Perhaps my mother was still grieving for our older sister, Christina, who was born odd. She was lost to scarlet fever when she was four. We knew the stories of how she was very beautiful, with golden curls and long eyelashes. She would embrace our mother, arcing her fingers like the moon, then suddenly beat her skull against our mother's nose so that it bled. She lived on peanut butter, slept for hours in our mother's arms or arranged fruit pastilles in patterns on the floor. She stood, rocking, on top of the black Lipp piano. She dived fully clothed into the white bath and paddled to the other end. Outside, in the paddocks, her eyes were caught only by the light in the waving trees and running water. When she disappeared once, she was found curled up in the dog kennel. Sometimes in the night I would wake suddenly, thinking I'd heard the wail of a child, caught in a white room, but it was simply the admonishing cry of a bird.

I grieve now for my dead mother, in her awkward beauty, her dark hair, her skin like a petal to touch. She was a warm presence in our daily lives. Mute with sadness, she often held me close as though I were precious. Sometimes she gathered Isabelle and me to her and held us both, each one against a cheek, and I smelled damp powder and lipstick. One parent survives the death of a child. One doesn't. My mother's face was so often glazed with loss. But not just Christina. Later there was something else. Some other grievance. And when the darkness of it descended upon her, as it often did, she withdrew into silence, a silence swollen with what I now recognise as a grief that was present but never given expression in words. I have had time to think upon it, and now see that there was something in our mother's life that would replicate itself in the lives of her daughters, and, without our knowing, it became the destiny of Isabelle and me to give our mother's suffering the articulation of action.

When death came for Christina, my mother called for poetry as another might a priest. She stopped playing the piano when Christina died. My father said that she had been so brilliant as a young woman that she could have made a fine career as a concert pianist. She taught Isabelle and me to play but I lacked interest, so she concentrated on Isabelle, who became passionate about music. When she reached a certain stage our mother took Isabelle each Thursday afternoon to a neighbour who taught advanced piano. She thought it better that Isabelle learn from someone other than herself. Isabelle said she had only a vague memory of our mother playing, plucking a sudden sadness from the music, her eyes closed or, if they were open, fixed on a point far out the window.

When Isabelle screamed to her that I had fallen from the Appaloosa behind the house, she found me hurt in the grass where I had been thrown. Dearest, she murmured and, lacing my arms about her neck, she stood me straight again.

Each day our mother enacted some private meaning, completely unknown to me at first. I wonder whether there is a particular moment when one becomes a bitter person. Or is it a slow accommodation to grief?

～

Photograph of the wanted woman, believed to be living in Paris. These words printed in *Le Monde*, and then my name.

My name.

My father had grown up with his father's stories of the war on the Somme. There was a photograph of him on the wall in the kitchen, entering Paris on horseback. He was billeted with a family in the place de la Madeleine. My father's favourite book was *Remembrance of Things Past*.

So I was Madeleine.

My father. My father was a tall, handsome man, with a loose ranginess about him. In the photograph I have of him in my apartment, he is standing by his motorbike, one hand on his hip, and his kelpie is leaning against his leg. His eyes are directly addressing the camera. When I look at him I hear the heavy movement of cattle on the peat, the smell of dogs, men, oilskins, grass; the shifting pitch and timbre of the sounds of the land, building to a crystalline stillness. I see the wind, the bleak sun and the glutinous white rolls of cloud.

He smoked a pipe, and when I first learned to walk I would follow the line, the trail of smoke, collecting his discarded matches. Here's another one, I would shout, gleefully locating a sign of him. Feather, just a pup then, wagged her tail so furiously that the whole of her haunches moved sideways. I smelled the tobacco on his sports coat, and in the tins and the neat, coloured pouches the tobacco came in. I studied the way he tamped it down into the bowl, the way his lips moved around the stem of the pipe.

Some evenings he read his Proust to us by the fire and these fragments were to remain always with Isabelle and me, and become our siren voices, calling us to longed-for places.

He taught Isabelle and me to swim in the brown river. We could feel the ebb and flow of him as he swam beside us in the water. He took his camera to the river and filmed us. I can remember seeing myself on film as a slight, brown figure with long, light hair, poised on the river bank, then Isabelle's arms flashing in and out of the water.

In the evenings my mother read to me from *The Red Balloon*. I knew all the words, but I wanted to hear her voice and see her fingers brush along the lines of words, and across the black and white streets as they traced Pascal's journey through Paris. She would tuck the blankets around my shoulders and I would feel the fleeting brush of her skin upon my cheek. I breathed the scent of gardenias and it remained for a second around me as she walked to the door and turned out the light.

～

Sometimes my father woke Isabelle and me as the light first showed through the trees, and we dressed hastily in corduroy trousers, woollen jumpers and riding boots. We caught the Appaloosa and rode across the land together with him before we were properly awake. I leaned my head on Isabelle's shoulder and circled my arms about her waist, still at some point in my dream that I was reluctant to leave. He showed us where maidenhair grew in certain places. The country had been cleared for grazing but there were swathes of wilderness here and there. On our Appaloosa, we rode with him to the far corners of the property to find this special fern. Together we saw rosellas, robber birds, brilliant blue wrens, flocks of lorikeets—flurries of birds that burst upon us like a cloud or fell in a flock, like leaves from a tree. The cattle were often caught too early to be difficult, and we guided their sleek backs until they were ambling in a group in front of Feather and the kelpies, along the channel on the slow journey to the yards where they were to be drenched or tagged. Their soft protests rose in the moist air, and they paused anxiously for calves to catch up and rub at their sides again. If a calf lingered, the whites of the cows' eyes rolled back in shiny black faces. I smelled the close odour of cattle and churned grass, and fell into the comfortable rhythm of the rolling walk of the cows, dignified in their movement, balanced between resistance and aquiescence.

Along one part of the river there was a stretch of ti-tree where wild cattle lived, sharpening their curling horns on each other and leading their own lives. Towards the west was a wilderness of another sort, with no evidence of human direction, all inpenetrable vines and tall trees, with just a little light stippling the treetops. Deer and fox lived there, and lyrebirds scratched in the dirt, their tail feathers shivering, falling down over them like a curtain, an end to something.

At midday we stopped in a scrubby clearing and my father squatted down to build a fire. He settled the billy on a nest of sticks and, when the water had boiled, Isabelle threw in some tea-leaves. I let them float on the surface a second before tapping the side of the billy. My father used a stick to lever the billy from the fire and, after twirling it to and fro, shifted the blackened lid a little to pour the tea into the tin cups we held out. We added sugar from a tin and knelt, drinking up the sweet, black tea while the fire died away. As we drank, my father told us about the shipwrecks on the coast, and some of the local history, like the great flood of November 1934 when the Fitzgerald sisters awoke in our old house to find spiders covering the counterpanes on their beds. Swamp snakes, quail and ducks sought refuge inside. That year the water didn't stop until it was halfway up the windows.

He told us that the house was built of clay bricks from the river by Chinese from the goldfields. Tarwin rose out of the swamp as the massive channels were built and drained the land, and rich, black soil was revealed when the blackwood, gum and musk trees were cleared. Before long, mushroom-pink strawberry clover buds grew where there were once only marshes, and the cattle were made fat, slow and sleepy from chewing it. From time to time the sky would become flat lead grey, then the colour of aubergine, and floods isolated the house and drowned the stock.

My father lit his pipe and, through teeth clamped on the stem, told us that Margaret Fitzgerald had lived with her sister Jeannie on Tarwin when it was a mansion. I could easily imagine the horse with the sulky stamping at the front door. In May 1952 Margaret disappeared in an icy gale that came in from Andersons Inlet. Despite wide and frequent searches, she had never been found. Our neighbours all said she had been murdered by a nephew, hungry for land. He lived on a neighbouring place called Madman's Territory. The name came from the family who used to live there and drank leech-infested dam water that had been sullied with the mercury used to separate ore and gold. The mercury sent them mad and it was said that at night you could hear laughing leeches skimming across the water.

We dashed the dregs of our tea on the remaining embers and climbed up on to the smooth back of the Appaloosa to continue our work.

Isabelle and I took on the task of finding the lady of the swamp. We hunted for her bones with the persistence that others used for their search for the thylacine across Bass Strait. We had great familiarity with bones because they lay about in paddocks quite innocently, blanching in summer. There were glass-edged skulls, the bones of animals that had perished somehow and been eaten by foxes. There were craniums, jawbones, snouts and eye-sockets. Their beauty lay in their detachment from flesh: bones held little fear for us.

We came to know the sound of the cattle truck rumbling up our long road before dawn, rocking across the old white bridge over the channel near the house. And we were there, waiting with our father in his oilskins and his felt hat with the ducks' feathers tucked in the brim. On his leggy piebald horse he mustered the slow Aberdeen Angus for the markets in the city, prodded their gleaming flanks.

Get away back, he called to the kelpies in the strangely encoded language of dogs, and they crouched, surged forward and paused, all to the rhythm of his voice, the tone of his command. They accompanied him everywhere as he shot rabbits, tore out thistles from his well-tended paddocks, sewed a summer crop of green peas, drenched heifers, and dragged calves with chains from the wombs of cows.

Once, as Isabelle and I were walking along our road, we were passed by a truck groaning with cattle. A breeze started up from the south and in sudden gusts of scent I smelled the mixture of black cattle, fear and diesel, and for the first time thought of that French word, *abattoir*.

~

When Sister Paulinus led the new teacher into our classroom we became perfectly still and silent.

Mademoiselle Fleury was French. She did not smile at first. Perhaps she was afraid. We could tell she had not been in Australia very long. No one seemed to know how she had come to be teaching French in a small town in South Gippsland in Victoria. There was something so completely foreign about her that it was compelling. People stopped and stared after her in the street. She was extremely beautiful but it wasn't just that. It was everything about her: her clothes, the way she wore the fabric as a skin, the way she moved.

Sister Paulinus entered the classroom and we all stood up.

Girls, this is Mademoiselle Fleury. She will be taking you for French, and the scholarship girls for private tuition.

Ariane glanced at us.

We are very lucky to have a native speaker, girls.

She looked away for a moment then, embarrassed.

I discovered that I had an ear for French and picked it up quickly. On Sunday evenings I polished my black school shoes, and rubbed a cloth over the smooth, brown skin of my school case, which smelled of books and ink. Stacking my books and pens inside, I set it at the foot of my bed, with the shoes resting on top. Learning French was like mass, but an intensely private ritual, celebrating words and beauty. For me it was as though Ariane had travelled all the way from Paris, bringing with her presents of language, literature and art with the sole purpose of changing my life forever.

Once I stood before my parents in the lounge room, fully dressed in my convent school uniform: the burgundy tunic, blue shirt, black stockings. I was ready for school. It was midnight and my mother looked up from her cup of tea, startled. Half asleep, I had risen from my bed, dressed and taken up my school case.

When I saw the expression on their faces, I realised the transparency of my ardour.

⌒

Ariane boarded in the yellow house with Mrs Teasdale, a severe woman who had a reputation as a careful seamstress. She had two rooms and her meals provided. Each day she walked to the convent school on the other side of the town and I sometimes saw her from the bus, walking in a leisurely way, as if she had all the time in the world.

In the distance, beyond her pliant, soft silhouette, a lilac hill rose above the green. The flatness of the area around this hill gave it the demeanour of a mountain. It was just as I imagined Mont-St-Michel to be, and every day, at this point in the journey, I lifted my head from my French books and studied the hill, noting any subtle changes in the light, the tones. Sometimes it was a deep aubergine, while on other days it was mottled lavender. As the bus turned into the town and the yellow house came into sight, I felt a tightening in my throat and was certain that one day I would go to France and visit such places.

The convent school was set right back off the street, in the heart of Tidal River, behind a hedge of photinias that were glazed with red in spring. It was built from sandstone, and next to it stood the church. There were netball courts and green ovals flanked by the Bald Hills far off in the distance. Above the entrance was the school's motto: *Faber quisque fortunae*, and underneath, in smaller print, the translation: *Each is the architect of his own destiny.*

Isabelle and I lived further away than any of the others, so we got on the bus first and we sat on the left-hand side. As the others arrived I looked up from my book, but not always. We had taken care to leave the back seat for the boys who liked to sit there and swear and smoke. They would have beaten us if we had taken their seats. Because of our books. Because we went to the convent school.

Youse are all up yerselves, they would say.

From time to time they would beat someone and the bus driver would yell at them in impotent rage.

I sat by the window throughout the journey, with my books upon my lap. I studied French. One of my books contained a map of the Métro, and it was this that I studied most closely, like a monk at a manuscript, as though it were an abstract painting that I was compelled to learn by heart: a poetic map. I memorised each line, the numbers and the corresponding colours that were spun like a web across the Seine. Mapping my future.

As the school bus made each stop along the dairy farms, one of the younger children ran to the roadside mailbox and placed inside a loaf of bread or a newspaper. And I whispered the names of each of the stops on my favourite line: number four, the pink one that ran from Porte de Clignancourt through Simplon, Marcadet Poissoniers, Château Rouge, Barbès Rochechouart to the Gare du Nord, then Gare de l'Est, Château d'Eau and Strasbourg St-Denis. It twisted from St-Sulpice around to Montparnasse Bienvenüe to Vavin and Alésia, and ended at Porte d'Orléans. Each little round stop on the line was like a word in a prayer that I chanted to myself on my journey.

My obsession with books was enough reason for the boys on the bus to beat me. But there was one of their group, a boy who smoked Benson and Hedges, who stood up for Isabelle and me once in a cool, dismissive way and they didn't bother with us after that.

That was my first lesson in the importance of appearances. He was different from the others. He got on the bus when it was already halfway through its journey and was crowded with bodies and school cases, cloudy with cigarette smoke. He was always dressed in full blue uniform, which he wore in a way that made you think that he wasn't bothered with his appearance. Yet I studied him closely and noticed that every inch of him was groomed. He was very fine looking, his teeth white, his nails trimmed, his sun-bleached hair curling at the ends on his collar.

When he got on the bus the others automatically moved aside, made way for him. The back-seat boys greeted him enthusiastically and offered him a seat, a light. But he always refused them and slowly pulled out a silver cigarette lighter from his pocket, then the golden packet of Benson and Hedges.

When he smoked it was as if he was enjoying the taste, concentrating on the smoke streaming through his lungs. He took his time and didn't speak to anyone. He never sat down but stood with one foot wedged against the bottom of a seat so that he didn't fall like the others when the bus swung around a corner; the movement of the bus didn't affect him at all.

Leave them alone, he said, indicating Isabelle and me, not even bothering to look at them. And they did.

I didn't know his name, or anything about his family or the farm where he lived. I didn't ask anyone or ever speak to him and knew only that there was something about him that cooled the ire of the back-seat boys, and that somehow Isabelle and I lived under the protection of his beauty.

By the time you read this

It's time to go.

With a start my eyes open in the darkness. I know that it's too early but cannot wait any longer. I wake in my single bed, which, years ago, I moved over to the French doors so that I could see out at night, and be woken by the moving morning light in spring and summer when the trees have hair. I have hardly slept. On my bedside table is a dictionary, placed there ready for the many *nuits blanches*, or in case I was woken suddenly by a nightmare. Reading dictionaries calms me. There is also the copy of *Le Monde*.

Rising quickly, I walk into my sitting room and turn on the light, which cannot be seen from the street. It reveals a small room furnished only with a red sofa and the credenza. On the credenza rests a purple teapot with a painted wide-eyed face, and a pair of dark Chinese silk slippers—a gift from Isabelle when she was in Hong Kong with Philippe at the university. There is also Xavier's postcard from his most recent trip to Australia:

> *There is wrestling in the middle of the day in this pub I am staying in. I love those two strange guys, especially Butterbean.*

He is so mean; everyone is cheering the other guy. But I'm cheering Butterbean.

Fumbling a little in my haste, I take up the postcard and photographs and look around for anything else I need to pack. Outside the window the Marais still sleeps silently in darkness. I moved here before it became fashionable and filled with little boutiques of designer clothes like the one just down the rue de Sévigné with a python living in a glass box set in the floor. When I first saw my apartment, I knew immediately that I would live here. The iron gate was decorated with chimeras and foliage; the staircase of dressed stone, with winding volute steps, rose in a perfect spiral. The white landing tiles were interspersed with seventeenth-century black cabochons.

From here there was the whole of Paris to choose from in the evenings after work. First a swim, then dinner and coffee before returning home to work on a new translation with the precision and the care for which I became well known. Sometimes I sewed my sampler. Armand thinks that I make dolls, and he gives me cuttings from his salon. I sew strands of hair, arrange them into forms that suggest letters curling like the script of an ancient manuscript; composing poetry of hair. It amuses me.

Because I was a teacher, an *assistant*, I was given a *carte de séjour* when I first arrived in Paris. After a year, and then standing in a queue in an office for hours, I was granted a *carte de résidence*, valid for ten years, and then another.

I am deeply aware of the pleasures of living alone and savour them each day, guard them rigorously. Not one of my colleagues has ever been inside my apartment. This was one of the reasons I hesitated to visit Xavier's apartment that first time. For I knew that a return invitation would be expected.

From the drawer in the credenza where I work on my translations for Éditions du Bois, I scoop up the small gifts Xavier has given me.

After the car crash in which both my parents were killed, when I had returned from the funeral in Australia, Isabelle had the credenza sent out to me because she knew how much I loved it. Our mother had died of grief long before the car accident ended her life. And since I had left Australia I had had very little contact with my father. Towards the end of the long flight to the funeral, I was sitting at the front of the plane in the silence. Most of the other passengers were asleep. A young man slid into the empty place beside me.

Are you awake?

He explained that he felt a great need to talk to someone, anyone, but everyone seemed to be asleep. He had spent all of the previous night, his last in Paris, sleeping on the grave of Jim Morrison in Père-Lachaise cemetery.

I listened to him. He reminded me of one of my students.

It was the most fantastic night of my life. Listen.

He handed me a pair of earphones, and I heard the sound of rain the colour of smooth slate breaking over me, then the soft sound of someone riding through the wet. Long after he had returned, satisfied, to his seat, I could hear the storm and the music, the beating rain, as I rode on the air through the night, towards Australia.

Some time after I had related this incident to Xavier, we were driving in the Compiègne forest and he surprised me with the long version of 'Riders on the Storm' on his sound system, which was actually more powerful than his car.

Riders on the storm, riders on the storm,
there's a killer on the road...

As the music boomed around me I had to ask him to stop because I was ill. He thought I had drunk too much champagne and he was driving too fast, and it became a joke after that.

No champagne for Madeleine. It goes straight to her stomach.

⌒

Inside my apartment I quietly close and lock the window that looks out on to the small garden in the square courtyard facing north, where I grow flowers around the old, cracked paving under the trees. In the spring I catch up the stray strands of the Japanese box and trim them with scissors.

The telephone lies silent. From time to time through the winter it rang in the middle of the night and I knew it could only be Isabelle. We were like two prisoners tapping between cells, and her whispers echoed from Katoomba. I recalled Ariane reading aloud in French the Jacques Prévert poem, 'Déjeuner du Matin', and the simplicity of the language making more poignant and cruel the lover's departure.

The abandonment, said Isabelle. That is the worst thing.

The French word *abandon* is a beautiful word when uttered: sensual and full of slow desire. But when Isabelle said it, when she uttered it, I felt the emptiness of the space where she sat in her wooden house in Katoomba, alone, with just her voice connected to me by invisible waves. Even before Isabelle rang me from Florence and told me that she had shot Philippe, I knew that she would break her silence.

She would do it. I could feel it coming. There was nothing else for her to do.

Are you afraid, there alone? I had asked her.

No. Not afraid of anything except my thoughts.

I will come, then.

No. Perhaps I'll come to you.

Now a letter has arrived with just a bare fragment of information, an address in Ravello. Just enough for me to go on.

Fear is looting my memory as I collect the things already set out, and put them in the small suitcase I draw from under the bed. Placing the photographs on the top, I snap the latch shut, brush my fingers across the credenza one last time and leave, softly closing and locking the door behind me. A line of light appears under the concierge's door. The concierge is the same woman who showed me the apartment almost twenty years ago. Short and square, she always wears exactly the same sort of clothes: a black skirt that comes to just below her knees, a black polo skivvy, black stockings and boots. In winter she adds a cardigan. She keeps candles in a hanging box on the wall in case of electrical emergencies, and is extremely diligent about her duties, sometimes sleeping in the hallway.

She is awake, but safely inside her apartment. I look up and down the street before slipping unseen into the rue de Sévigné, leaving the apartment where I have lived for all these years with the sights, smells and sounds of Paris as my salves and poultices.

I turn left and walk to the corner opposite the Musée Carnavalet, where Madame Sévigné lived, and from where she wrote those letters on the Chinese-lacquered drop-leaf writing

desk. My passage through these streets, the caryatids, entabla-
tures, mascarons, medallions and cartouches on the facades of the
houses, is the only farewell I can allow myself. In the dark, I turn
left again and walk along the rue des Francs-Bourgeois, passing a
window full of dismembered manikins, to the place des Vosges.

There is a grey wind this morning. Sometimes here there is
a warm wind and the lights are brighter at such times. Because it
is so early and dark, it is as if I am walking in my sleep, and what
I had to do in the dark is forgotten.

Suddenly a tree appears before me, exposing the paleness of
its skin, like the white of an eye. I am shocked by its naked form
revealing itself, and my breath quickens for a moment, until I
realise that it is simply a tree.

At number six, rue du Pas de la Mule, just out of the place
des Vosges, is the *boucherie* that sells musical instruments now,
not meat. There in the doorway is the metal gutter that was used
to drain away the fleshy debris of the day. One day the butcher
began hanging violins and saxophones next to his sides of lamb,
and before long the cold-storage room became a library of books
on music, and the slaughter rooms were workshops for restoring
instruments such as a silver etched guitar, a porcelain trumpet.

I enter the place des Vosges, where my feet crunch loudly
on the white sand. There are two triangular conifers at each
entrance to the *place*, and a grille around the grass. Setting down
my suitcase, I sit on a green wooden bench, waiting for something, but don't know what it is until flushes of rose appear in
the morning sky: when the sun rises I know I have been waiting
for the light. Perhaps it is also the symmetry of this Italian
garden I have waited for. The place des Vosges repeats itself, and,
looking deeper and deeper into the pattern of things, I notice
that each of the corners has its fountain, the black lamppost

curling down from the top where the lamp hangs; even the grates for the drains are evenly placed. The window boxes are full of double red geraniums, and in the evenings there will be a chamber orchestra or an acapella choir. Through the archway is the garden behind the Hôtel de Sully, surrounded by high walls covered in ivy. Along the walls are box hedges, and stone carvings representing the elements and the seasons. There is little in Paris that is unmanicured.

So early in the morning there is no one else here save the sleeping birds in the tangle of the linden trees. Fragments of the facades of buildings begin to appear. I have studied the round oeil-de-boeuf and noticed that each of the mansard roofs is slightly different. From my reading about Madame de Sévigné all those years ago, I know that she lived there also, behind the facade made to look like dusky red brick.

I am concerned only with that sensitive joy of seeing you, of having you as my guest, my father had said to Ariane on the night of their first meeting, surprising her, as he well knew he would, with his knowledge of Madame de Sévigné's letters. My mother averted her eyes from a truth that perhaps she already knew.

Something moves behind me. Quickly I turn around to see a man approaching. After a moment he whistles and a dog appears and scampers towards him. Watching everything, I rise and make my way through the Hôtel de Sully, out into the tiny rue de Birague, then left along the rue Antoine up to the Bastille.

⌒

Paris is a temple to my habits. The familiar architecture has become the backdrop of my days. I am not a fool. I know that such symmetry, routine and order leave me vulnerable to detection, but by ordering and structuring my life in this way, and rigidly adhering to habits, I avoid the trap of memory. I walk often, usually along the quai des Célestins. Sometimes I go to the *bibliothèque* a few streets away to work on a new translation for Éditions du Bois, which, along with the lycée, has employed me for almost twenty years.

In the reading room, surrounded by words in books, journals, manuscripts and cuttings, my muscles become relaxed, smooth and loose. Sometimes it's so peaceful in the reading room that I sleep in my chair and wake up to find myself staring at the painted ceiling above.

There are some evenings when my work gives me great pleasure. It is a soothing drink from the cool pool of poetry. I wonder whether a poem can be like a breath to the blue lips of the drowning. I am like an archaeologist, kneeling in the sand, sifting through my dictionaries for minuscule traces of meaning, tiny, precious shards of bones. Taking precise notes, I stop frequently and examine my work slowly, meticulously, alert for signs of a nuance here, an emphatic pause there. I am also like a painter, calculating the fall of light, describing volume and space through the relationships of hue. Each translation of a poem is like a picture. Some words make an alcove at the top of a flight of stairs.

Lately I have been translating an anthology of poems, the words of which are like lamps in the darkness. I pause at the post office and think of Isabelle and me, both wandering so far from home. I press some stamps illustrated with Picasso paintings onto a brown paper package and post the completed manuscripts in an envelope addressed to Éditions du Bois.

The Hôtel Salé is not far from my apartment. On my first visit there I came face to face with the *Madeleine* that Picasso drew in pastel and gouache on cardboard in Paris in 1904. When I arrived in Paris, still so young, I must have looked like this: the pink cheeks, the brown smudge of the eyes looking low, the hair tied in a knot at the nape of my neck, the nose a little raw from the approaching winter.

When I moved into my apartment in the Marais, I was aware of the irony: I had returned to the swamp. I added this to my library of ironies, the most recent of which being the discovery that in the eighteenth century, Mont-St-Michel had been a prison.

~

I can smell freshly baked pastry as I slip into a warm, bright patisserie on the boulevard Beaumarchais. A woman draws large trays from the oven. The cakes are put into little paper shells and placed on the glass counter.

Un café, Madame? she calls as I take a copy of *Le Monde* and sit in a straight-backed chair at a clean wooden table in the dimmest part of the room. My coffee comes in an ivory bowl and I eat a tiny rye and raisin roll. I am remembering an evening near here at La Zygotissoire with Xavier a few days ago. We went to the restaurant on the rue de Charonne, just the two of us, and ate sea bass, wild morels in cream, and drank Ladoix. This was before I had seen the photograph, before my contract with fear had been renewed. Xavier had looked over the top of his glasses at me. His foot tapped the floor and he told me of his immense happiness.

A man looks in through the condensation on the glass window of the patisserie, then comes in. He glances around and for a moment I think it is the man with the dog. I study my newspaper more closely as he walks purposefully towards me. He plants a cigarette in the ashtray on the table in front of me, and turns back to the counter. He takes a warm package smelling of pastry back out into the soft early-morning rain. As he continues down the boulevard, I watch him until he is out of sight.

I think I am going mad with the repetition, the old fears, and the horror of that. I am appalled to notice these feelings again: the fear of betrayal, of things being out of control, that I will do something simply to end the fear, to keep things as they are forever. More than anyone, I know that thoughts are actions.

The reason is perhaps because I have been free of love for so many years. There was never any attachment after the first few sexual liaisons of my youth. Just the soft kiss of a young German tourist when I was inadvertently caught on the Métro at midnight one New Year's Eve. With Xavier, it is different. When I am with him, the fear of betrayal, the sense of exclusion, that hidden current under everything I do, vanishes. But it must end or I will go mad. I must leave before anything happens.

The journey will bring me peace. I will give myself up to the comfort of motion. A journey will be a scaffold for my thoughts to hang upon.

I will be safe then.

The past

When I was twelve, my favourite room in the convent school was the languages room on the first floor, tucked away in the middle of the main building. There was a gas heater that warmed us in winter and on the walls were pictures of Paris. French novels and art books filled bookcases and a record player sat in a corner.

There were times, when working on our prose, that Ariane allowed us to play a Jacques Brel song, 'Ne Me Quitte Pas', while we wrote. If I lifted my head for a moment to the breeze that arose in the afternoons in summer, I sighed because there in that room was the whisper of another language, the promise of another world.

Ariane read a French tale aloud to us, about a woman who dreamed she was a cat and took her tail to the opera, up the flight of stairs. She held her tail up over her arm so no one would tread on it. It lay against her white arm, and the black velvet gown swirled back down the steps behind her.

As Ariane read, I studied her movements: all her gestures were in harmony with the air. Her oval face was wide and clean, slightly scented with a strange soap. She stood before us through the seasons in clothes that must have come from Paris with her. Their fabrics suggested flesh or skin. In summer she wore loosely woven linen dresses and silks that seem to have been cut particularly for her. In winter her dresses cleaved to her body, with the silk scarf falling from her shoulders in moiré patterns, as fine as the delicate skin of fish.

Unlike Isabelle, I did not have many friends at high school. They knew to leave me alone. It was unspoken. I did not have the time to do the things that were needed to cultivate friends, and I was always taking things too far, too quickly, not wanting to let things evolve in their own way. When I was tired of my own company I sought out Isabelle, whose friends tolerated me.

Ariane, too, was a little aloof from the other teachers in the school and the nuns. There was a cool irony, an austere and elegant melancholy, about her. She taught us with the same diffidence, but subtly acknowledged our various abilities, those things that could be developed and those that could not. She loved her native language and gradually we associated with our studies her sense of humour, the richness of her voice, the elegant cut of her clothes.

Sometimes she sat with her back to the sun coming in the window of the classroom, so that the light glittered through her earrings and we blinked up at her. Her fingers were sunlit, too, limestone white against the dark slate of the blackboard. I looked at the faces of the other girls, turned up towards her as she stood indicating the board. We were part of a warm, dusky tapestry, some exotic fabric in that afternoon light, a panoply of creamy peach faces, long necks, the flaming burnt orange of one girl's hair, the mustards and burgundies of the uniforms, our eyes fixed upon her hand. She held her tongue between her teeth when she laughed, and the bones in her face became visible beneath the skin. Her neck curved gracefully down to her collarbone.

I was as thorough in my study of her beauty as in my study of her language, and I began to research the particular ways in which beauty was constructed. I believed that it was something that could be learned, and that if my face was held to the light in a certain way I might attain this beauty myself. I examined Ariane closely: the fine texture of her skin, the shape of her lips, her hands, the cuticles like perfect shells, the line of her brow, her eyelids. I built up a picture of her out of layers of glazed moments.

Later, when things had changed, I realised that I had made her beauty the standard by which I judged myself. That was the lesson learned in that first year of high school: I believed that a woman's power was dependent on her ability to attract men, an ability that depended upon beauty.

Her face tilted up from the desk to look at me standing beside her with my exercise book, and I saw myself reflected back in the delicate veins of her irises. Her black hair was often caught behind her ears. It was so black that it was almost blue, like the sleek plumage of the sea raven, the cormorant. It was brushed back from her wide, clean forehead or it swung about her face and hung down across her eyes of peacock blue. It was cut all the same length. I noticed that the crown of her head was perfectly placed to create this curtain effect. There was a gap between the bottom edge of her hair and the top of her shoulders, and this was where her hair swung most luxuriantly when she bent over a book, a beautiful gesture.

~

In class, she told us in French of the lady who, waiting in her castle for her lord to return from Roncevaux, occupied her time by embroidering strands of her fine hair into a silken rope.

On the following day, at the hairdresser's, I saw Ariane's reflection in the mirror as she came in, smiling and greeting me as the hairdresser fussed about her. She didn't particularly glance at her own face in the mirror. I knew this because I was watching her, and, after she left, I stooped and collected a small, smooth swatch of her black hair from the floor. I put it in my pocket, and when I got home tied a piece of blue silk ribbon around it to draw it together to make a bookmark. I placed it carefully in the copy of Madame de Sévigné's letters that Ariane had lent me.

In our science class we were instructed to cut a small piece of hair from our heads, to examine it under a microscope, drawing what we observed. So one evening found me sitting up late at night in a circle of light in my room, books spread out before me, my notes at one side, and a dark swatch of hair under the microscope.

My research taught me that each hair on Ariane's head grew out of hollows called *follicles*. At the bottom of each one lay a garden of cells, the *papillae*, which nourished the fully grown hair. When they were forming a hair, the cells of the *papillae* multiplied and rearranged themselves to form a bulb. As the bulb grew, the cells changed, stretching themselves to become the hair strand, like the iris that grew from the bulbs in my mother's garden and looked like white birds from a distance. Each strand was composed of three layers: the outer cuticle consisted of hundreds of tiny, overlapping shingles and it was because they were lying flat that light was reflected and Ariane's hair shone in the way that it did. Pigment granules gave her hair its indigo colour.

Outside, in the night, a white bird perched on a fence post. My desk was near the window. It was really a table. My father said it was a *credenza*; a word that came from the Latin *credere*, to trust. In ancient times, a credenza was a table where food was placed to be tasted for poison before it was served. It had come from my father's family home, along with a little chest of drawers where I kept all my precious things. It was made of rosewood and someone had added several sections for holding letters. On the credenza was a glass jar that held the Giotto coloured pencils that Mr Garbini had given me. Above it there was a board where I pinned notes about my homework, photographs, leaves and feathers. My chair was made from the same wood and the seat was covered in bright red cloth.

Opening my heavy dictionary, old and smelling of foreign words, I took out my fountain pen from the tin that contained my pens and indiarubber, and translated each sentence of my French prose passage with precision, with attention to detail. These words became so precious to me that I wanted to sew them into the lining of a garment. I cracked them open like the shells of almonds or walnuts, seeking the soft, satisfying kernel of an idea inside. I worked on into the night, hungrily hunting through the dictionary while Isabelle and my parents slumbered at the other end of the long passage. A murmuring of birds was cut by the crake's impatient cry as it made its way down to the drenching purple and brown shadows of the channel, and the black cattle moaned outside my window in the darkness.

That night now seems a moment as transitory as the brush of a bird's wing upon my head: there was a simplicity about it that I have never experienced again. It had something to do with solitude, with love, and with words. If these things occur together, then you have something very powerful. If you then rip that away, the loss is the thing; the memory becomes as clear as a fossil kept in amber. You can hold it up to the light and see the past swelling in the rich nectar of loss.

In the late spring of that year there was only one day when the air was still. My father and I paused in the late afternoon and, as we sat on a log near the back of the house, looking at the dam far off to the west, I told him fervently of the new French teacher and what I was learning in my lessons. The air was infused with the perfume of cow dung and the smoke from my father's pipe. The metallic disc of the dam was a silver brooch in the landscape, and there was light on the edges of the Herefords, quiet at the rim of the water. We could see our dog, Feather, running, following a trail through the grass, each blade stroked by the shadow of the low sun. We watched until the dog ran off the edge of the landscape. I picked up my father's discarded matches, put them into my pocket and leaned against him as we watched the movement of birds. There were so few days like that, with its chalky luminosity. Usually the wind was there to be leaned into and struggled with, so I was not accustomed to the gentleness of that moment on the log with my father. We watched as a tide of colour came in and the evening sky was stippled with purples, blues and sepia tones. He put a hand upon my shoulder as he leaned down to pick a tuft of strawberry clover and held it up to my face so that I could inhale its sweet perfume. From the house came the sound of chords floating from the piano. Isabelle was playing the same piece over and over, trying to get it right. Again and again she struck the wrong note at the same place and went back to the beginning.

It was prize night. The French prize was a new Larousse diction-ary and Harrap's *Guide Bleu de Paris*. I couldn't hold them both in my hands because they were so thick and heavy with the things that I wanted to know. For a while I was the centre of attention and bathed in the warm glow of praise. The nuns glided across to my parents in the school hall at the end of the evening, offer-ing an ice-blue plate of scones laden with blackberry jam and clotted cream like paint in a pot. We stood there, a family as flawed as any other.

My father and mother were a beautiful couple. I had not realised this until the ball the previous year when in the evening my mother kissed my cheek, and brushed her soft, warm face against me, her motherskin smooth with powder, the luminous glass lying on her neck. She went off to the ball with a rare sideways smile at the self she saw in the mirror. I had never before seen her so happy. They were both dressed in black. I imagined them leaning as one to the arabesque of music, my mother's jewels flashing upon her neck.

When Sister Paulinus and Sister Maria introduced my parents and Isabelle to Ariane, I did not breathe. She appeared before my parents in black silk and spilled her warmth over me, and them, laughing into the circle that we all made. I was unable to speak as they were thanking Ariane for what she had done for me, asking her to dinner. My father touched Ariane's arm and said, I am concerned only with that sensitive joy of seeing you, of having you as my guest.

I was alarmed by the desire that arose between them, eclips-ing me and everyone else.

Nothing was ever the same again.

~

That night I was too restless to sleep. After midnight, I rose and continued a translation, using my new dictionary with the ribbon to mark my place. With my forefinger, I traced my name on the blue card attached inside the cover. I wrote the word *ambrette*, which Ariane had used that day in class. It was the name of an ambergris-scented pear. I tried out the sound of the word upon my tongue, swilling it about a little like a wine taster. Then I tried *absinthe*, a liqueur made by macerating and distilling the leaves of wormwood. And *couscousou*, a word that sounded to me like 'kiss, kiss', but which, Ariane told us, meant *becquetée*, or 'pecked at', from the food that a bird takes in its beak and rolls into small bits to feed its young.

It seemed that I could create beauty with the words I selected from the thousands there in the dictionary. Sometimes the right word eluded me; at others I captured it easily. Having another language meant an abundance of meaning, that the potential for beauty was multiplied. The words were like the silken shells of eggs, and I gathered them in an exercise book carried everywhere with me. I picked words up from my lessons with Ariane in the same way that I picked up stones from the river, and rubbed my thumb over their surfaces, dwelling on their smooth skins.

The shape of words, the way they fell upon the page, became important to me, as did the indentations my pen made on the paper. As each book was filled, I touched, with deep satisfaction, the backs of pages and their ridges of words. I was like a pearl fisher coming to the surface, bringing from the deep a pearl so perfectly round that it would roll about all day on a plate. Soon I had a secret cache of exercise books tied up with string and crammed with words, just waiting, it seemed, for sentences to string them on.

⤔

One Saturday that summer, my father and I rode to the furthermost part of the property to round up some Aberdeen Angus and move them into a fresh paddock. It was a long way from the house, past the maidenhair valley, on the southern side of the decaying wilderness, and we set out before light. After working with cattle and dogs all day we got off our horses and led them to Spring Creek. We found a hollow where bees' cries reverberated and insects were borne aloft in the rising currents of warm air. Sheets of cirrus clouds were appearing.

The horses stood loose, their long throats swooping down, manes hanging like brushed feathers. Their velvet noses dipped into the water where the river ran shallow and clear, over rocks covered in river moss, the sharpening breeze running across it like Isabelle's fingers across the notes on the Lipp piano.

Lightning flashed now and then beyond the Bald Hills, and the end of the day was pressing into the shadows behind us. The air was swallowing the light, and the stream began throwing up leaping trout. They flew out from plumed fans of water, gasping at the wild sheets of lightning, the violet rolls of cloud. The air grew turgid and seemed about to burst upon their backs, gleaming and flashing in the settling dusk.

My father walked to his saddlebag, where he kept the fishing tackle that had belonged to his father. In old tobacco tins were fly scissors, tweezers, line winders, pliers, spring hooks, gaff hooks, a knife and a whole pocketbook of fly hooks with their hair snoods, twisted gut traces. He took out a gleaming artificial lure, untied his Zephyr spinning reel, set it up and handed it to me. I threw the fishing line out onto the water and reeled it back, the lure spinning across the surface.

Between us we hauled out of the river enough fish for dinner that evening. Then we sat side by side without speaking, and watched the fish flying into the dusk. We hooked the trout, drowned now in oxygen, to our saddlebags and let the horses take us home before the storm broke, the kelpies and Feather at our heels.

Ariane came with the approaching night, on the bus at six, making her way through Feather's welcome on the verandah, bringing a green box of raspberries and exotic white blooms in her arms. Isabelle, who had been practising the piece on the piano that ran all through that summer like a melody line, stopped suddenly when Ariane knocked on the door and, when it opened, the pages of music, decorated with inscriptions, floated from the piano to the floor. For a moment we all looked at the shape of her cheek against the dusk as she was framed by the doorway, pausing on the threshold, appearing to wait for the room to give itself to her. The evening was made strangely luminous by her presence.

Ariane, Isabelle and I sat at the kitchen table while my mother prepared to cook the trout in butter in a pan on the Aga stove. The fish lay dusted in chalky white flour on a plate with a blue rim. My father chose, from the collection of cookbooks kept in the kitchen, a small book with a red cover.

He began reading: *To fry sillocks…*

Ariane leaned over to me.

What are sillocks, Madeleine?

We think they're like whitebait, I explained, having heard the recipe before.

My father coughed in a stagy way and we paid attention to him again.

The perfect dish of sillocks must be caught and cooked by the fishermen.

His voice grew warm and he looked over the top of the book at us. I could not see his mouth, but I knew he was smiling.

We ate the fish at the dining table draped that evening in pristine Irish linen. There followed the dark meat of a wild black duck and fresh mushrooms, picked from the broad open paddock that was furthest from the sea. Then green-gold pears poached in sweet white wine.

After dinner, my father led us into the sitting room to show Ariane his home movies. He dimmed the lights, set up the projector and arranged us on the lounge chairs facing the wall. Before the images appeared, the wall glowed in jumping light, then the film jerked, threading its way through the spools. It began, as it always did, with a series of fleeting, elusive, disjointed images of Isabelle and me swimming. And there was the pleasure of seeing myself through the eyes of others: a slight, brown figure swimming in the river. My long, blonde hair was darkened by the water or by the dimness that flashed in and out of the film: a staccato performance.

When I remember this now, I do not recognise myself as that child. I do not remember the comfort of being in that body, yet I can tell the comfort was there, and the grace. I stood tall beside Isabelle, and presented myself fully to my father's camera.

My father was telling Ariane about the film in his precise way. He located it in time, in place, in our history.

The last film was a newly developed one. Some neighbours' children were throwing a ball about in the driveway that led up to their old farmhouse. There was a seductive burst of lush grass and the shadows of giant pine trees sprawling across the hard-packed road. A figure reached into the picture from ragged edges to retrieve a ball that had rolled into the rose garden. She threw the ball to Isabelle.

It took a few seconds for me to realise who it was. It was the clothes that I knew first. I saw a girl of twelve. She was too tall and bony, her hair cut short in a rough bob, high back on her forehead. She was awkward in her movements as she ran for the ball, so lacking in grace that she grimaced when she saw the camera and she was freeze-framed, distorted before being dismantled by the searing light of burning celluloid as the film snagged.

I looked away from the screen in shock, my face flushing. I had not seen myself so. Within the space of a couple of minutes I had realised two things: as a young child I had possessed a simple grace and beauty; at twelve it was lost to me.

Mon cœur

At the Café Charbon last night Xavier ordered the *ortolan*, a small songbird from the south of France where he was born, a delicacy that tasted, he told me, of a mixture of truffles and foie gras. Purists ate it whole and still aflame—beak, feathers, bones and all. Although he was completely engaged in eating this creature, perhaps he noticed my discomfort, the way I looked away from him after Sophie, the publisher at Éditions du Bois, came and spoke to me.

She was extremely elegant in the way she walked and the way she removed her coat; entirely self-contained, with a stillness that reminded me of a pool of water under the moon. I liked Sophie but, because of her appearance, had always remained detached. Our relationship was completely formal.

At first I thought I had misheard what Sophie was saying to me as Xavier poured her a glass of red wine. But no. Someone, possibly an Australian, had come into Éditions du Bois and asked about me. Just that day. She could not be sure whether she had done the right thing but he hadn't seemed like a friend, so she had not given him any information. She hoped there wasn't a problem. I was able quickly to change the subject. My translation was almost ready and I would deliver it soon. This pleased her.

I was afraid I would give myself away to Xavier. If his hand had been resting on my wrist, as it so often was, he would have felt my pulse quicken a little as Sophie spoke to me, a little sweat starting, a trembling in my clenched hand as he bent politely towards me. It was, at first, just a small electrical spark of memory. One would have to know me very well to realise that there was something wrong. I made an effort to gather myself privately, to soothe the blood roaring through my head, the shaking of my limbs.

It breaks my heart to leave Xavier. But I must leave him before he discovers that I am like belladonna honey, and he is not safe. Already he must suspect that Sophie has said something that has upset me.

He could never understand why I declined to go back to Australia with him, although perhaps he suspected that there were things I had left behind and would be happy never to see again.

We could go on a holiday there, Madeleine, he said in his quirky German English. I don't like Spain very much. The weather and the sea are wonderful but the rest is thick and strange. When George Sand was there with Chopin she wrote a true thing: *They hate us.*

He told me tales of his Australian journeys. There were photographs of a coastline somewhere, of a group of his colleagues standing for a camera under a wider sky than you ever see in Paris. I refused bitterly. Australia? No. I put the photographs down on the table and suggested that perhaps we would go dancing that evening at the jazz club.

Ah well, it must be the Côte d'Azur, then. We'll find a Dufy window for you in Nice and sit at it. Then when you get bored we'll leave behind the faded grand hotels along the Promenade des Anglais with their odalisques on the walls. We will invent paradise.

Already I could see a balcony tiled in mauve, orange, violet and yellow ceramics, a tangle of greenery like Bonnard's *L'Atelier au Mimosa*. The soft prisms of the roofs. I longed for sun so hot it made me shiver.

I hate the beach, so I will sit and watch you swim, continued Xavier. I'll carry your surfboard, perhaps. You won't like the stones by the sea, though. I know about that. You will stub your toe.

He didn't press me about going to Australia after that. He accepted it as gracefully and completely as he accepted many things about me. As if just loving me was enough for him, as extraordinary as that might seem. He wasn't to know that I had built my life on a flood plain.

This is the way it is, the way it has always been. I have struggled with this, been vigilant about my vigilance. Nothing in my behaviour has escaped my scrutiny, particularly when I am with Xavier.

At first I had believed that, with Xavier, I was free of fear at last, such was the intense passion I felt for him. And he for me. Something found its centre, its balance, in each of us when we were together.

Absolument, Xavier often says. He is so sure of everything about us, so confident. When I found myself at such peace in his arms, I was moved because it seemed that I was free from threat, after all. Feeling such peace in the presence of another human being was something not experienced since I was twelve, when I had spent an early morning riding with my father and Isabelle. Just the three of us with the horses and dogs. Before it all came undone.

It breaks my heart to leave Xavier, to forgo him. But I must leave him before I am discovered, before I am hunted down. For if he discovers the truth he will leave me.

I am sure of that.

Memory bell

In the twilight of that first time Ariane came for dinner, it was agreed that she would come and ride the palomino, Queenie, who needed exercising. Queenie was the most beautiful of our horses, with her flowing mane, large eyes, and slender legs so quick to take flight. This arrangement happened without my having to orchestrate it. My mother suggested it, some wound she was tearing at in herself making potent her collusion with my father, and she quietly disappeared to her room after dinner, not to return.

Late that evening when my father drove Ariane back to her yellow house, I sat between them in the car under a spray of stars forming, aligning, as we jolted over the corrugations in the dirt road. We passed wires strung silver between poles like strands of hair. Their conversation swam about me like the light of the headlamps searching ahead of us in the darkness. Something about the way they spoke to each other was alarming: it didn't include me. I was there between them, but not there at all. I had not read the books they spoke of, each tossing titles over my head to the other.

It's so strange, Ariane said seriously. I have not spoken to anyone in this way. You are the only person I have met in Australia who knows these books.

My father was at his most charming, and when he said her name it sounded different from any other word I had ever heard him utter. As the journey continued deeper into the night, I felt myself subside quietly, like the side of a mountain slipping from itself in flooding rain. I was transparent, like an X-ray; there was no substance to me, just bones blocking the light a little.

My father was quiet on the way home and eventually, having been hypnotised by the red eyes that shone on the white guide-posts along the road, I slept on the broad, bouncing seat.

~

The clothes that Ariane wore for her first riding lesson were completely unsatisfactory, my father said, laughing at her as she arrived on the six o'clock bus from town. He took command. Before taking Isabelle for her music lesson, my mother shyly offered Ariane the use of some jodhpurs and a riding shirt and boots that she no longer used. When I came out of the house and swung on the verandah post, eating a biscuit, my father was holding Queenie still while Ariane climbed up upon her back. She turned a moment to smile at me and laugh at herself. She hunched her shoulders to indicate her ineptness, and I caught my breath, thinking for a moment that it was my mother there, leaning against Queenie's warm flank.

~

Ariane gave me extra tuition in order to prepare for the scholar-ship examination. During those private lessons after school on Thursdays, before her riding lesson with my father, we studied books that weren't being studied by the others. I waited all week for the hour when I would sit at her table, holding my breath beside her, with the books set out in front of us. They were special books, because they belonged to her, not the school, and her name was written on the flyleaf of each one. She allowed me to take them home and in my room, late at night, I examined them carefully for clues to her life.

She had written a date and the name of a place inside each book. These words and numbers were like a tiny, intricate pattern, woven or etched, small, repetitive like some mysterious code I wanted to understand. The date she had purchased it? Or read it? And the place? Most of the places, I knew, were in Paris, but some must have been when she was holidaying. There was the book of Madame de Sévigné's letters with *Nice* written on it in a larger, more relaxed script, and I learned a new way of pronouncing the name of the sugar biscuits Isabelle and I ate with milky tea after school. This new way sounded of the sea.

She also lent me a book of photographs of Paris. In the diffuse light of the city, I imagined Ariane's form against the background of these photographs: in the Tuileries she rested upon a stone seat; at Les Deux Magots I could see the wicker weaving of her chair, the metal table behind the glass of the window; she wore sunglasses, and a scarf. The little white cup and saucer. Always alone. She even read her novel with her sunglasses on. Without moving.

⁓

In class we were studying Raymond Radiguet's *The Devil in the Flesh*. I was, by this time, enthralled. Ariane folded her arms and cradled her elbows in her palms as she spoke of the story. She walked to the window and looked out. It was simply the sound that the word made when she said it. Ariane said *l'amour*, and it was as if she'd opened her mouth and spoken under water.

The lover

I check the street outside the patisserie, board the bus that pulls in, and take a seat. It makes its way through the Bastille and on to the Gare de Lyon.

It will be hard to leave, to start again in Ravello.

This morning journey is giving me the time to sort things out in my mind, to think about the unthought, to seek constraint and containment. For looking at my life just now, I am not sure what is in front, what's behind. The edges change, as happens at the line where one colour meets another—a third appears. I want to consider the situation carefully until it's straight like the raked pebbles in a Japanese garden. Perfect.

Under a car, a black cat with yellow eyes jumps back in fright, blinking in the fumes of the bus. The man beside me absently chews the aerial of his mobile phone.

I know I will get some sort of job in Italy. I am a good translator and teacher, reliable, hardworking, dedicated to my students, and have a flair for French. My accent is good and I can create a certain shrug of the shoulders. I practised these motions as a child: the hand sweeping back the hair, the shoulders swinging as I walked along the street. Sometimes I would look down, then up, suddenly, so that there was a dramatic quality to the way I moved, a half-smile on my face.

Isabelle said that French had gone to my head. She said this when she came upon me cultivating the gestures of Jean Seburg in front of our mother's mirror. It is precisely what an older sister would say to a younger one. Now I long to hear Isabelle's voice saying such things to me.

⌒

I wake after dozing a little as the bus moves through the morning. A woman is getting on and as she takes the seat in front of me, her hair laced with blue ribbon swings out from her pale neck over the back of the seat.

I notice a person's hair before anything else about them. And if there is something fine about their hair—the colour, the shine or the shape—then I am anxious to observe this for a while, rather like the man who loved ponytails. He would haunt the hairdressing salons of Paris and offer women money for their ponytails. He would do the same to women he met in bars, offer them a thousand francs for their ponytails, and if they agreed he would produce a pair of scissors, snip off the ponytail, put it in his pocket and leave. Later he took to sitting behind ponytails in the train and doing it illicitly. He used a new pair of scissors each time, so that you got the feeling that the preparation was the important thing to him, the purchase of the scissors, and the planning.

The bus stops again and others board. I scan their faces, but find nothing to fear. The journey provides a place for my thoughts to rest. For often my thoughts are like flocks of tired birds that have moved together across continents, and need a settling place: my thoughts have strained against the winds, turned in tight circles above the sea.

The light is coming through the bus window more strongly now, so I take out the copy of *L'Amant* I always carry with me, wherever I go, so that if there is an unoccupied moment I will not dwell on thoughts of the past. I can draw it out and open it at any point and read.

One morning in July 1984 I caught sight of its face reflected in the shining wood of the dark shelves at Galignani's bookshop on the rue de Rivoli. When I took it up, my hand swept across the textured white cover and my thumb felt for the thickness of it. Standing there, I began to read and grew breathless with the beauty of its language. I was anxious as the woman took it away from me to place it in a bag, and walked from the bookshop directly to a cafe by the river, where I continued to read. The waiters kept coming and I ordered coffees. Then they stopped coming. They realised that I could not leave until it was finished. Reading that book was like being in the sunlight. When I paused to order coffee, it was as if the shadow of a cloud passed over me. The water sparkled on the other side of the river, where the sun still shone strongly, and I knew that I had to wait, that the cloud would pass and it would be warm again, the words like blood flowing once more in my body. The light fell across my hands as I smoothed the clean, white pages. A busker played a violin amid the din of lunch being prepared, ordered and served as I sat, not looking up, reading on, page after page, oblivious to the river, the avenues, the thickening crowd. By the time the waiters had changed shifts the words had pressed their shape into me forever.

That autumn I saw Marguerite Duras on a television program, waving her rings and bracelets in the air, and I wanted to kill her because of the way she revealed the ruthless intent of a child's heart.

⌒

As the bus pulls in to the Gare de Lyon, I slip the book in my coat pocket and gather my things. I walk across the road, past the *boucherie* with its bodies of white, naked flesh hanging from hooks.

Inside the *gare*, I purchase a ticket for Rome, then Naples. The man tells me that I will have to buy my ticket for the Circumvesuviana when I arrive in Naples. He is speaking loudly and I glance behind me, quickly take my ticket. I put my suitcase in a locker. Apart from the credenza, my belongings have always been few, and are light, easy to catch up so I can run for a train at a moment's notice. They are safe for the moment and I am able to attend to my next task.

I sit at a table in the station cafe, draw out the pen, writing paper and envelope I have brought. I hesitate a little. It is twenty-six years since I last contemplated this action. It has taken a long time for me to repeat it, but now I am threading the narrative curve back to its beginning in a quiet script. This letter is more difficult to write than the first. Perhaps this love is so deep because it is underscored by loss—the shadow in my brain somewhere, like a phantom limb. This is one of those times when there is a detachment working within me: snipping, snipping at the threads that sew me to the day, snipping from underneath the cloth. Then I notice that the cloth itself is slipping, unravelling.

But there is the journey I must make. It is what I know, this leaving in the night. It is how I have lived my life. It's too late now to change. A terrible sadness lowers itself upon me. It happens sometimes. It can begin with something as simple as the touch upon my hand of a hair falling from my head. It is unreasonable and swells inside me like an organ gathering water into itself after the body has been attacked by a cancer. It fills my chest and my face and makes it difficult to breathe. There is little use in telling Xavier about it because it would lead to that other telling.

Apart from Isabelle, there is nobody else.

Sometimes I tell it to the grey river as I walk along the quai d'Orsay in the evenings and watch the barges from the bridge. I have wandered away into the dark wood. And returned alone. Despite all the love, it was not enough. It could never be enough.

Suddenly I am weeping. I put my sunglasses on and write the letter. I do not pause and it flows from my pen. I remember every word as though it were yesterday.

I catch the train to St Denis. I am early, so I go into the Stella Artois brasserie, where I am not known. The man behind the bar nods to me and I say, *M'sieur Dame*.

Un café. Un, he screams to the air and gives a little bow.

Unbuttoning my black coat, I make my way to the back room, past the local workmen in their blue overalls, and sit at the table in the corner, facing the door.

The only other person there—a man sitting at the table opposite me—twists into his chair like a corkscrew into a cork. He throws his food from one side of his mouth to the other and sniffs loudly.

The walls are blackened by cigar smoke, the air heavy with the odour of Gauloises and garlic. When the coffee comes in a small blue cup, I hold my hands around it.

The brasserie begins to fill with people who are also on their way to work. None of them takes a seat. They throw back their coffees, grab a bite to eat and dash back on to the street. Amid the backslapping and jocularity I shiver a little. There is a gravelly American voice on the radio singing about cashing his chips in Rome.

I leave some francs on the table and walk across the road to the school. An old couple on the other side of the road is in trouble. The woman is about sixty, thin, and wearing a long-sleeved grey sweatshirt with blue terry-towelling track pants. It is clear from her bone structure that she was once extremely beautiful, but now the skin at her elbows hangs like a shawl from the bone. Her hair is wispy, patchy. She is slumping over the fence, slowly disintegrating. Her husband holds her with one arm, a trolley crammed full of groceries with the other. As I reach her, the woman comes to rest on the footpath. Her head rolls on to her chest and I kneel down to her. There is a strong odour as urine flows, pools around her. She slowly becomes aware again of her surroundings.

She's just finished chemo, her husband weeps. She's just come out of hospital. I told them it was too soon. She is losing hair from her soul.

Afraid of someone stealing the food, he takes the trolley to their car and leaves his wife with the strangers who are collecting about her now.

Her fingers curl, clutching at my hand like a baby's. Her gaze turns in shame away from the ugly mess she is lying in. Someone from the Stella Artois brasserie says that they have called an ambulance.

Is there anything you want? they ask.

A tissue?

I draw a handkerchief from the pocket of my black coat, and give it to her, but she looks at it and sobs. It is too beautiful. She will not use it.

Mist coats the air, muffling the scream of the ambulance.

As the ambulance people arrive I notice that she has still not used the handkerchief, despite the wet mess on her face, that she holds it—a fold of serene, soft blue—delicately in her left hand. It is the handkerchief with the rolled edges that Xavier gave me.

Her husband returns with a gendarme, and I quietly slip away. I almost go back to ask her whether I can have the handkerchief back.

I am ashamed of this.

~

No one else has arrived at the school yet. I hear the faded bark of a dog and the other sounds that are caught up with it as it travels along the backs of buildings by the cemetery behind the school. I will have a little time to make some preparations. It must not be anything too noticeable. There is not a lot to do. Even after almost twenty years in the same place, I have not let down my guard as far as work goes. My classroom is neat and orderly; my record books and files are up to date. I have not lost the habits of a person who is aware that she might suddenly have to leave.

My departure will not result in the chaos that one might expect. There are many unemployed teachers and translators in Paris. I am sure they will find a replacement quite easily. Someone will be grateful for the work. In fact, my actions might change for the better the fortunes of a whole family. With this in mind, I make my last preparations.

My students are technical students. They spend a great deal of their time down in the metal rooms, the engine rooms and the woodwork rooms. They come to me for English conversation and 'culture'. This week I have been looking at Australian poetry and they are learning some poems in English. Last week we were reading English technical manuals for washing machines. They are mostly young men in their late teens and early twenties who will be employed all over France, perhaps in the nuclear power stations that rise suddenly out of blank fields in the country. Although my students enjoy their English lessons, their attention is really upon the grinding and clashing machines on the ground floor. I realise that I will not see them again.

When I first came to Paris I stood like a tree, bare in winter. The sky was oyster-grey. I had packed the dictionaries and Harrap's *Guide Bleu* in a suitcase not much bigger than my old school case, and left Australia, flying over the pale patches that were salt lakes. From above, I watched the land wash away.

I had saved all my money carefully while studying. The knowledge that I planned to leave for France forever as soon as possible, and make that city of a thousand bookshops my home, was like a secret in a silk sack that I wore between my breasts. I obtained an exchange in a school in Paris for one year, with a small salary and a room in the school. I arrived in September and was due to return home to Australia the following September. Isabelle had married Philippe in August and, eager to visit his childhood home, they promised to come.

It was simple to alter my surname in Australia before I left, so that all my documents showed a hyphenated name, the first of which I quickly discarded once I arrived in France.

Paris was the light at a paper window, and I knew I would never go back.

~

Paris first appeared to me as if in the flashing scenes of an old movie. The shadows of the trees made the sunlight dip in and out as the taxi delivered me far from the mansard roofs, to the *lycée technique* in St Denis. My room was on the third floor of the school, at the end of what were once students' dormitories.

I was the only person living on that floor. My footsteps echoed as I moved about. Below me was the Spanish *assistant*; above me, the German. On the first floor were the concierge and his wife. Outside the window of my room the fractured view showed the backs of buildings and a cemetery with fragile black angels slipping out of frame. Another cemetery lay to the north.

Double death, I wrote to Isabelle and Philippe.

On my first day there I stood looking out the window. A fly lodged in a web on the shutter; a dog leapt about a man as he stood urinating by a grave.

A dome of grey cloud pressed down upon St Denis for months at a time, and as I walked the pavements quilted with leaves I saw the feet of a hen or rooster lying by a tree, indicating the sky; the broken necks of bottles. St Denis was the grimmest part of Paris, especially the Sarcelles, a place reeking of urban misery. The monarchs lay in the basilica, in the midst of this disarray. It was only Isabelle and Philippe's visit that made that first year bearable for me.

In the evenings I left my room at the lycée and went into the centre of Paris to visit brasseries, cafes, the busier the better, for then I could watch people living their lives and study the ways in which they did it. I explored subterranean Paris. The tunnels of the Métro and Catacombs were an unseen world, like a dark, nocturnal unconscious—a mirror image of the city that lay above.

All along the Left Bank were posters of the Belgian artist Folon, and his pale images floated past me during my first months, like moths caught in a light that was too bright; the world was abstract, distilled to just shape, form and colour. I was an exile there.

I wore dark clothes, dyed my hair jet black and bought a pair of heavy, dark-framed spectacles. People would sometimes turn and look at me on the street. They were usually tourists who would want to take my photograph because I was so tall and looked so French. I told them I was born in a tiny village near Versailles and that I mentioned Versailles because no one had ever heard of my village. A management school operated there, little else, so when I found a hundred-franc note one day, lying in the dirt in the grounds of the palace, I bought a train ticket and came to Paris searching for *la vie parisienne*.

I told them such things in English with a distinct French accent.

In summer I wore sleeveless linen dresses and read *Le Monde* in cafes. I cultivated a taste for jazz and Gauloises. It was all windows, mirrors and the river. I moved on from the cafe if people started to try and get to know me too closely. I tried out Patricia's words from *Breathless*, the film I saw when I was learning French, and, because of all the practice, knew the exact rise and fall of these words, the way to move my mouth and head.

There were endless opportunities to shrug and say, *Je ne sais pas.*
In those days, not having yet learned the security of routine and
solitude, I welcomed disguise and practised carefully the delivery
of complicated statements, seeking the correct grammatical
construction, pronunciation.

When the job at the school began, it all changed and I
quickly gained confidence and spoke the language freely and
energetically, though many of my original habits remained.
Perhaps they were the habits of a stranger in Paris, but they had
become such a part of my life that it was simpler to continue.

Now, instead of making my way to the dining room for lunch
with the other staff, I leave the school, head across the place
to the Banque Nationale de Paris and draw out all my savings,
kept in an account under a false name. The clerk screws up
his eyes and looks closely at me, surprised by the amount of
the withdrawal, the fact that I am closing my account and
changing my money into Italian lire. Perhaps he suspects a
hidden purpose.

A problem?

But no, certainly not, I tell him. I'm having a little Italian
holiday.

I tell myself that although I will be carrying a good amount
of money, for I won't be able to use credit cards, I now pass
unnoticed quite easily in crowds, and that because of this it will
be fine. The money will last a long time and then there will be
a job. I tell myself that I must not be afraid. I have known what
it is like to be really afraid, and I know that I will never feel that
way again.

Entering a cafe of glass and polished mirrors, I draw out a small, square table and sit on the banquette, my back against the wall. I harvest a field of thoughts, conjugating a future—a truce with myself forged by Isabelle. Taking out the envelope that arrived two days ago, I read the words: *via San Francesco 2, Ravello.*

I order a *tartine* and a glass of wine and see the headlines of a newspaper lying on a nearby table. There has been a dreadful train accident in Germany. Much suffering. I remember sitting in the dining room of the school eighteen years ago when they told me that the news of the morning had been full of a train accident in Australia. I couldn't understand then the name of the place, but bought a paper later and read about it. Sydney. A suburban station. A train had derailed, hit a bridge, and many people were killed or trapped in the wreckage.

The staff at the school were clearly surprised at my lack of reaction. Australia so rarely featured on French news bulletins that they had been quite excited by it. They wanted to show that they were identifying with me. A shocking thing. I nodded, but didn't want to know any details. After that I never watched television and sold the one in my apartment. I rarely listened to the radio and carefully avoided reading newspapers, training myself in this way for many, many years so that it is completely natural for me now.

A car rolls in front of the cafe. The driver, a very beautiful woman, tries to pull into the empty space there. She has run out of petrol and the car will go no further. Another car approaches and appears to be about to take the parking place. The woman leaps out of her car and abuses the driver through his window, then rushes to the front of her own car and vainly tries to drag it into the space. A group of young men, who are passing, assist her.

Laughing, they drag the car and position it into the space. The other car roars off. The woman thanks the young men and they set off to buy petrol for her, not wanting to detach themselves from her beauty. I take advantage of the noise and movement to leave the brasserie.

⌒

As I make my way back to the lycée, I feel some shame that I have avoided Xavier. Today he had wanted to plan an outing like the one when he took me to a quarry to find agaric, a family of fungi that grows on tree trunks and in caves and on decayed wood. Later he would sauté them in butter in a shallow pan, and dress them with herbs. Another time we went to the Jardin des Senteurs off the rue des Morillons. We made our way through the wisteria, lilac, lily of the valley, the honeysuckle, the plots of chamomile, vervain, tarragon, thyme, laurel and sage. He took my hand and ran it over the labels in braille. The Beehive School was nearby and the vines of the pinot noir vineyard, and peach trees. Towards the lake there were heaps of stones.

Used to be there was an old slaughterhouse there, he said, pointing.

He aimed the camera at me.

Stand still and look at the photo-machine, he said.

And then he shot me.

⌒

I sit in my office, writing a short note to leave for the principal, explaining about a sudden death on the other side of the world that requires, regrettably, my immediate and ongoing attendance. My mark book is open in front of me and I will make the final entries so that it will be completely in order for my replacement. There is a sound and I start, my pen jerking ink onto the page.

As the door swings open, Xavier's figure appears in the glass. He comes in, stands before me. He has been hurrying and there is a smudge of light on his forehead. The lenses of his glasses are fogged with disappointment. Removing them, he rubs them with his sleeve. His tie has flown over his shoulder and his hair is unsettled. Today he is wearing a rich blue shirt. He looks at me with a strange smile floating about his lips. They tremble a little with desire. Looking up at him, my thoughts are of spine, skin, muscle, my consenting mouth; his hand drawing a line along my belly, up between my breasts, then spreading out there and stroking me languorously; then the fusion of beings for a moment.

What's happening with you this evening? Do you perhaps want to come to the rue de Médicis? I thought a roast would be the thing.

I smile. He knows that I will eat only the vegetables and he will salt and oil them with extra care. He doesn't know that it will be my last meal with him.

Of course, I will come after my swim. How can I refuse such an offer?

Good. Some special coffee I have found for you. It's flavoured with roast figs. I think you'll love it. I'll see you then? About seven?

Before leaving he kisses me, straightens my collar and glances at my mark book, his voice gentle now.

You work too hard, Madeleine. You shouldn't miss lunch like that.

When he has gone back to his classroom, I am quite alone again and left thinking that I cannot leave him. But I have read in *Le Monde* the report of the discovery of a body in South Gippsland, Australia, believed at first to be the missing lady of the swamp who had disappeared from Tarwin in 1952. But they were not her remains at all. Another disappearance many years later involving a woman, a French national. Dental records had identified her. The photograph of Ariane beside the one of Isabelle and me. The older sister, it said, was wanted for the murder of her husband, a writer. There was a description of the younger sister, who was the last person seen by the landlady in the company of the French teacher. My name.

⌒

Everything changed when I met Xavier. They say that falling in love is the only form of madness we enjoy. I fell in love with Xavier against my will. For many years everything had been just so—in order. Xavier disrupted all that and, at first, I almost resented him for it. It was as though he had snatched my map away and I had become lost, disoriented, forced to rely on his sense of direction.

I heard his voice before setting my eyes upon him. Feeling someone studying me across the lunch table at the lycée, I was tempted to say, as Patricia had to Michel in *Breathless*: I'm going to look at you until you stop looking at me.

I was reading the catalogue of an exhibition I had seen. Under the glass of a large tabletop *vitrine* were sixty-five tiny dead birds delicately laid out in rows on folded white linen. Each was dressed in knitted garments such as were usually made for newborn infants, their feet and beaks protruding. I had experienced a grisly fascination with it and had to force myself to move away to the next exhibit.

Madame Grangier was placing white sugar onto a small mound of yoghurt. Madame Arné was opening a bottle of beer with her strong fingers for Monsieur Jules, the workman, who sat with his colleagues in blue overalls at the other end of the table.

I knew only that there was a new professor of French.

It was the fine patina of his voice that first attracted me, and the strange twist his German mother had given to his English. He kept his eyes fixed upon me.

Do you know how it is to eat a pomegranate? he asked me.

I was irritated by his attention. The others knew and respected my preference for remaining silent and reading while dining. They rarely interrupted me. I considered him over the top of the pages, frowning. He was a large man. There was a deep crease in his chin, a half-smile on his face. I looked down. He held in his hand a piece of fruit so beautiful in its design that I thought that it should be drawn, rather than eaten. It resembled a magnification of human skin. The roughly sketched lines of orange and red curved into gullies, crosshatched at the point where it rested in his hand. I could imagine the way it would bleed when sliced, when the scarlet beads of tear-shaped flesh were broken. The beauty of it moved me but he wasn't going to know that.

Very carefully? I replied, raising one eyebrow.

He smiled at that and introduced himself. When I took my hand from the pocket of my overcoat and gave it to Xavier, he placed his other hand over it, held it a moment as though it were a gift. *Un petit cadeau.*

After that I was aware of Xavier's presence in the school and, with annoyance, noticed myself listening for his voice along a corridor, through an open window. The odd thing was that Xavier was often out in the foyer when I arrived at school. Perhaps he had looked for me at the window.

I am not a beautiful woman. There is a plainness about me that makes me invisible to both men and women a lot of the time now that I have discarded the affectations of my youth. If things had worked out differently in my life, I may have found this a great sadness.

Xavier's attention to me was unusual, a threat to my solitude, my safety. He unnerved me further by correctly identifying my accent immediately. Most Parisians believed me to be English or American. I didn't disabuse them. It was of no consequence to them.

You are Australian, he accused me, smiling, familiar. It wasn't a question; he knew Australia too well for that. But a surprise. As though he had come across some small and rare marsupial that had never before been sighted in these parts.

For Xavier, it seemed, I was an object of cultural fascination. My Australianness was the thing. I knew I should have been more careful, but he insisted on deepening our acquaintance. He had made many trips and knew my country very well. When he was younger, he had stayed in Sydney for a year, lived and studied at the university, and had become an expert in Australian culture, even acquiring an Australian accent. He laughed when I confessed how hard I had worked to lose mine. And I laughed at him when we occasionally spoke English together. He was the only Frenchman with a German accent mixed with a strange Australian influence I had ever met. Every word seemed to end with the murderous *eye* of the crow calling across a wide, empty paddock.

Xavier had grown up in the south of France in a hotel, where he passed a lot of his time at the top of a spiral staircase in a little tower known as Maximilian's Tower, after his maternal grandfather. He would say things like: Let's sit and watch this storm.

He lived in the rue de Médicis near the Jardins du Luxembourg, across the Seine from my apartment in the Marais, and worked at both the school and the Sorbonne, specialising in Australian history and literature. Xavier had planted a eucalyptus tree in his garden. Because it was a snow gum, he thought it might survive. That was how I first came to visit Xavier's apartment.

Would you like to come over and visit my gum tree? he asked.

That is the thing that is so unusual about Xavier. He makes me laugh. In fact I have noticed that, in his presence, there is an aspect of my voice, my laughing voice, that I have never heard before, a rich depth that is without bitterness.

Once we were having lunch under a spreading pin oak in the Café Bon Ton near the Panthéon when we heard what the woman at the next table was saying to the one-armed man with her. You know, I hadn't realised before now that you're left-handed.

As we leaned towards each other in silent amusement, the waiter approached and pointed first to the gathering clouds overhead and then to a table behind the glass of the cafe.

That's for you both, should you require it.

Deep in conversation, we were the last to notice the rain coming quickly in large drops. We hurried across the shining flagstones, through the cloudburst and indoors. From our table there, through the glass, we watched the storm break. Everything was green, lush and dark. The rain beat down upon the deserted metal tables.

Outside, through the drumming rain, a sharp, brittle breaking sound came and a white plate, falling from a waiter's hand, smashed to pieces as he took flight, a collection of glasses and crockery balanced on his arm. As the storm increased in intensity, a second waiter ran to help him, a drink tray held over his head for shelter.

Suddenly, urgently, I turned from the window and touched Xavier's elbow. He moved his head towards me, his face animated, his eyes demanding mine.

There's something I should tell you, I started to say. But at the moment I spoke, thunder cracked directly above our heads, and the building shook.

What did you say? he asked, leaning forward. I shook my head, regretting my words immediately, and a drop of rain flew from my hair onto his lips. Before I had realised what I was doing, I had raised my hand and reached forward to brush it off. He caught my hand in his, held it by the fingertips, and kissed them, his eyes still upon mine.

After this, with great trepidation, I went with Xavier to his apartment in the rue de Médicis.

He was at a sort of resting point in his life: he lived alone and had done so for long enough not to feel the need to explain why. Outside his building was parked an old red car. At the entrance a priest passed by us, his neck stretched ahead of him like a tortoise. I saw Xavier make a movement to mimic him, then control himself in mock horror at his own unruly behaviour. We rose to the third floor in a very small, dark metal cage. I was acutely aware of his proximity and touch when his arm brushed against mine as he held the door back for me. We entered his apartment, where light streamed into the room like water. I could see only light and wood for a moment, until my eyes became accustomed to the brightness. Out of the corner of my eye I caught an odd, furtive movement. A large, red-feathered parrot was hanging, like a diver ready to fall, from its perch in the cage near the window. It was watching me closely.

Who is there? Who is there? it screamed suspiciously.

This is my companion, Bluey, he said and I smiled at his adoption of the Australian habit of calling any red-headed person or thing blue.

We sat at a round table and drank a Coonawarra Merlot together while he told me about his love of the wines that came from the *terra rossa* there. When he was preoccupied he rubbed his thumb against his forefinger, as though feeling the texture of his thought. He waited for me to speak, assuming that I had something to say. He was transparent in his actions, articulate in the way in which he poured the wine, easy to be with. There was in Xavier a sure balance between insouciance and tenderness. He ambled about in fine-grained leather shoes from Cordoba in Spain, disappearing to fetch something that he thought might amuse me. He had a vast collection of dog ornaments, some of which he drew from their shelves to show me. He described the different dogs he had kept over the years, the last being a borzoi.

When she died, I buried her there.

He pointed across to the Jardins du Luxembourg.

I had to sneak in at night, but it means she is in the family still.

He suddenly leaned close to me and I held my breath as he reached out to touch me. Instead, he pulled a long, white hair off my coat.

A little reminder remains there and here, he said.

While he was out of the room a moment, I was able to study it more closely. It was much larger than looked possible from the outside. Perhaps two rooms had been made into one. It appeared to have been recently renovated. The floors were oiled wood. Large, folded-back French doors looked down to the Médici fountain in the gardens. Two walls were lined with books and I rose and walked over to look at the collection of fiction, history, art. All Australian. As I shivered a little, he walked back in.

Are you cold? Would you like the doors closed? This spring in Paris is a very good joke; it could be a winter; only the flowers give some signs. It's horrible! This is the second spring in line who was not a spring. We had some minus degrees in the night.

Down below, people were walking about in the Sunday sun, over the white sand and down into the sunken garden. Toy sailboats were moving across the octagonal pond. The scene was like a Seurat painting, with points of light and colour that individually merely pleased my eye but when constructed by the brain as a whole took on shape, order and meaning. I found myself disaffected by this, preferring the meaningless scatter of light not defined too rigidly. Seurat regarded each of his paintings as a temple and the figures and shapes in those paintings as columns in the temple. He had a mistress called Madeleine who, after his death, disappeared from Paris without a trace.

Someone glanced up at me from the gardens. Instinctively I moved back from the window, turned from the light and joined Xavier at the table again.

He offered me a little cake, a friand.

I should have bought some *petites madeleines*, of course, he laughed. Bluey loves them too.

He said later that he thought of the expression *esquisser un sourire*—to give the ghost of a smile. That's all he got from me on that day.

Often during those first few meetings he was engaged in a monologue. Then it was as if he opened an aperture in the sequence of spaces in my silence, and I joined him in the dance of conversation until there were times when I forgot myself completely. There had been so few moments in my life when that had occurred. I remembered those early days with Isabelle and my parents, or going sailing in Australia with Isabelle and Philippe years ago when I was lost in the pleasure of the moment and being with them. They were happy, lying together in the shade of a tree by the dam, and their happiness embraced me. Then they took the sailboat out in the thickening summer breeze, and just after I took a photograph of them I smelled rain and there arose a wind that took up the little boat and sent it rushing across the water. The boom swung at Philippe and plunged him off the back of the boat into the water. I watched in horror as Isabelle reached down to drag him up. He drifted away safely in his life jacket while the wind took her in the boat and smashed her up against the bank far away on the other side of the dam.

From the beginning Xavier was straightforward in his court-ship of me. It was as though he knew immediately that he loved me; as though he was quite accepting of this fact, not afraid of it at all. He said that when he found me he was able to suspend his disbelief. Something about you, Madeleine, has been lost in the translation. I see it is my task to find it.

He has been the unravelling of me, and I had hoped for an exorcism. My initial suspicions persisted for a while, though—perhaps Xavier was writing a book on Australia and would want to be with me for the information I could provide.

I am ashamed of such thoughts when I remember them now. His love has complicated things greatly. It has brought back the fear. I felt it recently when, on the Métro, I sat with Xavier in the pushdown seats at the door. There were the suede faces, the soporific trance that enfolded regular travellers. As the alarm sounded at the next stop, the door flew open and a man leapt into the carriage, landing on his knees at my feet. He made the sign of the cross and begged for money. After I gave him some coins he handed me a piece of paper that uncurled in my hand and read: *The souls of the dead come back as birds.*

The letter

On an early-morning ride with our father, the button grass, driven by the wind, looked like white caps on the sea. Passing by a hump of black trees on a deep green rise, I urged the Appaloosa into the dark patch of ti-tree where tall mangroves blocked the cold light.

This was the place where the swamp still remained, and everything was older than anywhere else. A bleak space. Brittle folds of paperbark peeled from the ti-tree and fell into the dark water. Swamp birds feasted on insects, and crakes lived and bred here. The trees were black up to where water had risen and remained, trapped until it had become dank.

Listen, Isabelle called, and we heard a muttering of birds, a moan along the ground, the grunt of a waterlogged black cow, stricken, prostrate, lying broken in a circle of mud where for a week she had tried to gain her feet.

My father slid from his horse, slapping the leather, a flash of knife in his hand, the muscles tightening in his face. I saw the white of the brain where he cut before the blood. The silence in that dark, wet place was cold and, eager to leave it, we guided the horses back out into the light. As we rode close together on the Appaloosa beside our father, Feather at our heels, he explained that sometimes decisions to end a life had to be made quickly, unexpectedly; that sometimes it was the only thing to do.

The horses paused on the edge of the pink wood of maiden's blush in a clearing in the middle of the bush. We heard the language of birds that seemed to call a name, the sharp 'kirrik-kirrik' of the spotted crake as it flew low over the clearing and settled nearby. The light played on the combination of feather and wing, illuminating a bill of olive-green, a face dotted with red eyes and black flanks barred white.

Our father leaned over and put his hand gently on the bridle at the mouth of our horse. In the wilderness we were three figures: one in light, two in shadow. He stilled our pony and pointed, a finger to his lips. A fox was standing motionless among red and yellow grasses, a beautiful apparition created by the smoking sunlight. We saw him before he saw us. He started sniffing about, and when he caught our scent he shivered but did not look our way immediately. As if he did not want to acknowledge our knowledge of him. When the impatient Appaloosa jerked away from my father's grip and executed a capriole, the fox shot into the darkness of the scrub.

⌒

Every Thursday afternoon, after my lesson with her in the yellow house, Ariane caught the bus with me. When we reached Tarwin my father would be waiting for us with Queenie and the Appaloosa already saddled and we rode out together. He was teaching Ariane to ride, much as he had done with Isabelle and me. He was firm but gentle and careful to make sure that she enjoyed herself. Sometimes she tossed her head in frustration and my father laughed at her impatience. She was a quick learner and soon she was even able to ride bareback.

One warm Thursday afternoon, the three of us rode to the wide, brown river under an undulating canopy of white silken cloud, the sun gilding the horses' eyes, the paddocks hazy with summer heat. My father was leading Ariane and me to the swimming hole through country that had a lushness then. We were shining in our swimming costumes, our bodies slipping on the backs of the horses. I sat balanced on the broad back of the Appaloosa, its legs, knee-high in grass, kicking up seeds that remained about us in a haze.

We heard the sound before we saw anything. It sounded like breathing. It drew closer like a dragon exhaling. From behind us, there appeared a giant red balloon carried aloft by the air, drifting like a feather in from the open country to the north, accompanied by a few fair-weather cumulus and looking for a place to land. Small figures waved from the swinging gondola. The horses shied and my father struck up a faster pace so that he was just ahead of us. Our horses pricked their ears and started to trot after him.

Out in the middle of the empty paddock, as the balloon disappeared, my father started to canter, and we tightened our legs and sat back into the rhythm. I glanced behind at Ariane. I saw that the strap of her swimming costume had slipped down from her shoulder and her breast was floating free. It was creamy, opulent, and moved apart from her body. I turned away until, from the flush on her face, I could tell she had noticed and adjusted her strap. Then my father started to gallop and we followed him to the river, in flight for a split second during each stride.

Once at the river the horses stood in the shade, grooming each other's manes. My father sat on the river bank under the wild apple tree, leaning against the trunk, his shirt sleeves rolled up to a place just above his elbows, which rested on his drawn-up knees. Between his lips he rolled a long piece of dry grass. His brown felt hat was pulled low over his brow, so I couldn't really tell whether he was dozing or watching me swim in shafts of sunlight in the brown swell of water as warm as milk. Ariane dived in to join me, her limbs moving in one fluid, continuous motion. She swam through the liquid gloss of the river, making longer and deeper strokes, pausing then gliding forward on the faint swell she had created. Her luminous hair floated on the dappled surface, shaded for a second as birds passed over the river.

Afterwards we rested on the sand, surrounded by the cloying perfume of the honeysuckle. Ariane looked like a shell on the beach, so smooth were the contours of her body, so still did she lie.

⌒

I showed my French teacher the photographs from *The Age* that I had found in a box in the pantry: Margaret Fitzgerald was a tall woman in a long gown, an abundance of hair around her face. There was a photo, too, of the three sisters, with Margaret sitting on the left and Jeannie off to the right of her. Behind them stood Flora and a cousin. Another photograph showed Margaret as an old woman wading through the swamp in gumboots, one hand holding up her skirt and coat. Hopping through the water beside her on slightly higher ground was her dog, Warrigul.

One day I arrived for my lesson at the yellow house a little early. Ariane was not there, so to pass the time I looked at the books on her shelf. There was a collection of photographs by Man Ray. It was not among the books that she had offered me. It was a slim volume with a black cover. As I turned the pages quickly, pieces of women's bodies flashed at me, a pastiche of erotica dislocated from bodies, isolated on the page by the camera. There was manipulation and a submission to the photographer. I saw breasts lying upon an opened blouse, shocking me with their shape, their diffuse eroticism. Then canna lilies, their petals like folded flesh. And a face. Nothing between the eyes and lips, just a clean expanse of pure, white skin against saturated black. I closed the book guiltily as Ariane arrived.

On the evening she took the scholarship students to see *Breathless* at the cinema with the tin roof, Ariane wore a turquoise silk dress with a sea-wave pattern. I heard the rustle of her dress as we sat down. It was just a small group of girls and a couple of parents. She said it was important that we saw the film, as it was part of a movement called *nouvelle vague*. I was a little drunk with the pleasure of sitting between my father and Ariane, excited by the novelty of the jazz score, the quick cutting in and out, close-ups, the wide angle of the camera, and the jerky, compulsive images on the screen. Disjointed pictures showed Jean-Paul Belmondo standing in the middle of Montparnasse.

Patricia quoted from Faulkner: *Between grief and nothing I will take grief.* Michel chose death because he said grief was a compromise. When Jean Seberg turned Jean-Paul Belmondo in to the police at the end, I thought I could hear the sharp, splintering sound of shattering glass.

My father sat up very late alone that night, smoking on the verandah. He had *Remembrance of Things Past* on his lap, but he did not turn on the light. I could see the embers flaring in the dark when he drew on his pipe, smell his tobacco in the air.

Towards the end of that summer, my mother had arranged to take Isabelle and me to see Mr Garbini and meet his niece who was visiting from Italy. At the last minute I decided to stay behind to work on a translation I was anxious to perfect for Ariane. They left, both annoyed at my stubbornness. My father had ridden away early that morning, saying that he would be working stock all day far off, near the river.

Alone in the house, I went to a drawer in my mother's dressing table and drew out her hair. It lay in the box from France that my grandfather brought back to my grandmother after the war. The long, black braids were tied with blue silk ribbons. Taking two hairpins from the crystal tray under the mirror, I clipped a braid to each side of my head, behind the ear. I moved my head back and forth so that the plaits slid heavily across my back, my shoulders. I folded the hair across the front of my face so that I could smell its dark, earthy scent. Carefully, I tucked my own short hair behind my ears so that the braids looked as though they belonged to me. This was a ritual that I usually completed at night as a young child if I woke suddenly and went to my mother and father, afraid because the moon was full and the white sheets were shaking themselves on the clothesline outside. My mother would distract me, soothe me, by saying I could take out her hair.

This day, though, I went further than I had gone before: I untied the ribbons and loosened the tight braiding until my mother's hair fell freely about me. And in the mirror I could see my mother's cheek. Disturbed by a slight noise, I quickly tidied the hair, replaced it in its box and slid it back into the drawer before leaving the room.

Outside, Feather rolled onto her back on the verandah and I threw sticks for her to fetch, then climbed the walnut tree and sat in its branches and smelled walnuts and leaves that were dying. Seeking with my teeth the little wrinkled brains of nut flesh, I cut my tongue on the sharp splinters of walnut shell.

I was passing by the window of Isabelle's room when I heard a sort of tapping sound, echoed by a pluck of fear in my brain. I had believed myself to be alone at the silent house. I leaned over the garden bed so that my fingers on the windowsill were taking the weight of my body, precariously balanced. I heard the sound again and tasted sour blood in my mouth.

The curtain shifted a little in the breeze. A diaphanous shroud of white cotton, it floated out onto the windowsill, touched my fingers lightly, brushed over them, then sank back inside the room again as the breeze let go of it. In the centre of the room stood the round rosewood table with the bowl carefully filled with flowers. Isabelle had placed them throughout the house just that morning after gathering them early in the garden. The dark shades of blue, green, lavender and copper made a glowing iridescence. Perhaps one of the roses had fallen. I could see the raw skin of a rose petal on the table. Perhaps that had been the sound I had heard.

The breeze began again. The sky was gently swelling with grey, and the poplar tree let loose a blizzard of leaves that turned towards me in a rush. As the curtain moved I saw further inside. My glance flashed in the dim room, and the image remained in my mind, the geometric severity of it, the bones of it constructed there. The walls were pale with the skin of poplar tree shadows.

I strained my eyes to read the contents of the room. Two figures lay on the bed amid rumpled sheets, striped with branches, the grey corners of the room reaching out to the warp and weft of limbs. There was the insistent hum of desire. A half-seen face, a shiny, dark head pressed into my father's arms. In the second before I drew away from the window, I heard the sound of my father's voice.

My heart was a clenched fist.

At the Prom, my mother, father and Ariane went down to the creamy silk sand of Venus Bay, where sea and beach formed a smooth curve that contained, subdued, the movement of the waves. From a weathered wooden post hung the iron bell that was still sometimes used to summon help when a ship was driven onto the rocks in the bay. My father's eyes were strangely lit by the reflections of the sea. Our mother, in dark Sunday clothes, moved a little apart from the other two and looked out to sea with her Jackie Kennedy eyes, scanning for disasters that might lie beyond the horizon.

Isabelle and I went up through the smell of hot vegetation to the sand dunes. With the sun flinching in the waving seagrasses, we pulled at Feather, buried ourselves and the dog in sand, and spied on the three figures moving slowly in waves of light by the shore. My mother was further along the beach now. She paused a moment, and raised her arm to shelter her eyes as she looked into the sun across the sea. At her feet the sea foam was littered with the remnants of boats, oars, ossified fish forms and emaciated driftwood. From her isolated figure I looked back to where my father and Ariane had also paused. They lingered together, looking down at something they had discovered in the sand. Ariane bent down to pick it up. She overbalanced a little and we heard her laughter rise and disappear again in the wind.

It was the fact that they did not touch that gave them away.

With a sharp cry I leapt up and, scattering sand over Isabelle and Feather, ran down across the squeaking sand to the sea. The adults watched with Isabelle as I waded out and dived into the stark, cold sea, the surf stripping down my boneless white body.

⌒

The next day I found a nest of cracked birds' eggs blown down from the palm tree, lying like a wreath on the ground near the house. It belonged to a dark brown swamp harrier. I had seen the bird, with its white rump, long yellow legs, the barred tail and wings, hunting rodents, wheeling over the tall grass, the reeds and rushes, diving from high above. Into the twigs and shredded bark of the nest was carefully woven a strand of shiny black hair, a careful fragment of information that I drew from the nest and studied under the microscope.

The screen door snapped and my mother's shoes appeared in front of me, the heels worn down. I reached out to touch them but she moved to the laundry, a basket of washing pushed up against her breast.

My mother stood in the steam in the laundry. I saw wads of clothes and bedsheets on the floor. Her eyes were swollen. Red blotches soiled her face. In her hand was the stick she used for beating the clothes in the boiling water in the copper. The air burst with washing powder. My bones flinched at a grief I did not understand.

Far off my father was herding cattle to shelter from the coming rain.

Why didn't you want to go with him, Madeleine? That's not like you. You could still catch him if you leave now.

But I had taken out my exercise book and was carefully drawing the hair, so perfectly constructed.

⌒

Ariane gave us a lesson on silk production in Paris. The place des Vosges, she told us, where Madame de Sévigné had lived at one time, had originally been designed for the manufacture of silk. She described how a piece of raw silk was placed on the table to receive its colours. Indigo was crushed in a sandstone tub and then used to prepare madder, to make a deep red dye. A final indigo bath made their tones particularly tempered and deep—the mellowness, matt surface and sombre reflections of madder silk.

The word *madder*, of course, entranced the class, but particularly me, as I dipped further into the colour of the heart.

⌒

The sky was a cold, sulphurous yellow all the next weekend. In the home paddock near the machinery shed, Isabelle was speaking to a sheep. We had heard our father say that he would kill that sheep. It had been separated from its flock, and their bleats were like the guttural voices of chanting monks. Isabelle could not bear the death of any animal and was looking deeply into its gentle, ovine face. She thought that it was important for the sheep to hear a human voice before it died.

Nearby, a tree stump was mounted on three legs, ready. In the shed were choppers, saws and knives of various sizes. On the wall was an illustration of the cuts of meat, a sheep divided into its eating sections: baron, saddle, loin, rib chops, shoulder.

I wondered how it felt to be chosen for slaughter.

When my father approached, the sheep knew. Again and again I had been a witness to this, and my inaction made me a participant: each time a sheep was killed, Isabelle and I suffered and tried to hide this suffering because we knew it was weak. Other people did not seem to experience it—not the children of our neighbours, nor the girls at school. My father was not aware of this suffering in each of his daughters. It was something completely foreign to him and would have galled him had he known. He had taught us to ride and shoot. It was a natural part of life in the country.

The yellow tincture of the sky deepened. The sheep was impassive as my father dragged it on its back to a worn patch outside the shed, Isabelle and I trailing behind him. It was a large sheep and when it began struggling, trying to break away, my father lost his footing for a second and half fell on the hand he had put out to steady himself.

Get hold of it, Madeleine.

I held the animal against my leg the way that I had often seen him do, not unlike the way a shearer held a sheep when he shore away the wool from its belly.

My father had sprained his hand.

You do it, Madeleine. I'll tell you how.

The sheep moved against my leg. I did not speak to the sheep. I knew that I could not speak to this doomed creature.

My father adjusted the animal, took hold of my arm with his good hand, and showed me the way you turned the head so that the neck was stretched back, exposed. The sheep struggled again suddenly and almost escaped my grip. I knew from the guide set out in my father's Coopers Notebook that the heart of a sheep would normally beat seventy-five to eighty times a minute. As its eyes reached backwards, I could feel the heart beating much faster. The sheep began to pant as my father gave me the large killing knife, which he had sharpened that morning. Isabelle had closed her eyes and was holding her breath, but she did not move away.

I dug the knife into the neck and held fast with my other arm as the sheep kicked and screamed. Soon the scream became blood and shot out in a spray of violence onto the dirt. I did not let go; I finished the job. When the animal no longer moved against my leg, I let it fall to the ground and untied its legs. My father stepped back a little and told me exactly what to do. Because I had seen him do it so many times, it was easy for me to slide the knife down under the bone into the breast of the sheep and drag it down the belly so that it sliced open. I handed the knife to my father and reached through the steam into the creature and paused a moment, holding the heart in my hands. There was a moment of gratitude at the warmth I found there, for it was a cold morning. He gave me back the knife and, as the heart slipped in my hand, I gripped it firmly and sliced it free. I threw it aside, as I had seen my father do, and the butcher bird waiting on the tree jumped a little in anticipation. It proffered its long, hook-tipped bill. The dogs, trained in detachment, crept forward while averting their eyes from us.

I slipped the knife under the wool and through the skin, making a *stch*, *stch* sound as I skinned the sheep, stripping it down to a carcass. My father helped me lift it onto the hook in the shed so that it was easier to peel the skin away, which

I did by whipping the knife at the fine white fat that attached the skin to the body. It tore like paper that had been glued to a surface, my fingers feeling, here and there, the texture of bone. I finished, and could tell that I had done it well, and that he was proud of me, but for the first time in my life I did not care. The killing, the day's slaughter, had merely sealed me off from my father forever. Beside me was the sound of Isabelle's twisted breath. I turned to her, giving him my back. The knife lay where it had fallen on the ground, and the dogs licked hard at the dark bouquet of dried blood in the dirt.

Later, in the ambiguity of twilight, Isabelle and I crept out of the house and climbed a swaying gum tree. She rubbed my hands hard with the lemon-scented leaves, but I still smelled the flesh and the sour blood of the animal on my hands and apprehended my terrible collusion with my father. It was against this that the course of all my following actions were set.

⌒

Sometimes we heard my mother weeping in her room when she thought there was no one around. Once, when I went into the bathroom after she had been there, I looked down into the ceramic toilet bowl and saw blood. Much blood. I rushed to find Isabelle and showed her, pointing.

Our mother's heart is bleeding. It's fallen through her body there.

Isabelle stepped back, shocked. She didn't say anything. As my anger swelled into a dark cloud, I tried to tell her what was happening, but somehow it didn't eventuate. Just as I wanted our father to tighten his grip upon my mother, not let her slip away like that. But he didn't, and she did.

One morning when I was out on the Appaloosa, searching for the fox, I discovered the burial place of the lady of the swamp. I had been riding all morning, but the fox eluded me, so I tied the reins to a tree with vase-shaped flowers growing from its branches, and set about building a sharp stick fire in a depression in the damp ground. I buried some potatoes in the embers and sat beside them, waiting for them to cook, watching the clouds scrolling across the sky. Feather was tracing deer and fox with her nose. She shifted some leaves and disturbed the shard of an animal, one of her own. She whined a little, growing more interested in the soil and the other bones that lay there resting with stones, curdled in the dirt. I pulled her away and noticed the remnants of a dog collar, a long, narrow bone, too long for any animal I knew. Carefully I pushed aside more leaves to reveal, in a small garden of bones, the remains of the lady of the swamp, lying curled around her dog, Warrigul, where they had ended together years before.

On my return home I removed my gumboots by the back door on the verandah and carefully leaned the tops over so the spiders wouldn't enter in the hollow time of night. My mother silently placed food on the table. I told no one of my discovery, not even Isabelle when she asked me where I had been so long. I watched my father eating, and bent my head to my own plate, busy with rogue thoughts. The Aga breathed gently into the kitchen and the warmth shifted to other rooms. Betrayal formed in my mind until it was like a mosquito bursting with bloody promise.

On the following Wednesday, the day before Ariane would come to us after school to continue her riding lessons, my father pointed to the sky and said there was a flood rain coming. He instructed me carefully to tell Ariane not to come.

Be sure to say that I will ring her to make another time.

He said it with such transparent sadness.

The next day I was tired in class because I had been writing all night. Ariane and I were studying the letters of Madame de Sévigné because they were widely regarded as an exemplary model for the epistolary genre. Her husband was killed in a duel in 1651, and following this her daughter Françoise moved away after her marriage. Madame de Sévigné's letters to her beloved daughter were full of news, events and gossip. Her natural manner of writing, the conversational tone of these letters, had, Ariane explained, provided an insight into the nature of French society at that time.

As I sat in my room that night, contemplating my task, I grew sleepy and allowed my eyes to close and my head to rest on the table. Upon waking I saw that it was very late. I studied my notebooks, picking out words that I had collected and hoarded.

The next day I went to school full of my plan. Everything depended on the letter.

⌒

Mrs Teasdale answered when I knocked on the door of the yellow house. She asked after my parents, and led me to where Ariane was waiting for me in her room. I placed my books and pencil case on the table near a blue glass jug. I picked up an ornament made of eggshell glass so fine that it felt merely as if something had brushed over my hand. Around the room were the shelves of books evenly stacked in tight lengths, a tilted mirror. I imagined what would remain in her room and made a mental inventory of the objects that would point to her absence: the silver-backed hairbrush with some strands of hair laced along the bristles, the white cup and saucer half drunk, things she had collected on her travels like the preserved duck egg covered in volcanic ash, a pearl shell from coral reefs.

Ariane indicated the chairs and table, and I sat down and we went through my exercises. When we had finished I asked whether she could help me and showed her the letter. She read it twice and looked at me a little quizzically. I told her that I had found it in a book from the library, and asked her to translate it for me into English. I handed her a piece of paper.

She glanced at her watch quickly and took it from me. She wrote out the letter in her green ink, in slow, ambiguous arabesques. She wrote, paused and wrote, and when she had finished she smoothed the sheet of paper and read it aloud to ensure that she had been accurate in her translation.

Dearest

By the time you read this, I will be gone. I dreamed of snow last night and knew that I must go.

Let me tell you.

My soul stood like a tree, bare in winter when I came to this foreign land, my heart askew, like a bird flailing across continents. I did not expect to find my resting-place here with you and kept our love like a secret in a silk sack that I wore between my breasts.

Like a monk at his manuscript, I have studied you, and the gift that you are. You are the light at a paper window.

You have reached the centre of me, opened me like a precious letter. I travelled with you in the night and will not forget the journeys that we took into the deep heart.

I am with you there always…

Ariane was thoughtful for a moment, then a smile animated her face.

It's quite beautiful, Madeleine, isn't it?

After the lesson, she asked me to wait while she changed and collected what she needed for the riding lesson. I told her that my father and I were going to show her where I had found the lady of the swamp. I could see that she was anxious to be gone. Dressed in my mother's jodhpurs and white shirt, Ariane returned to the sitting room and, picking up the brush, she stroked her hair, so that her face was concealed by the dark hair for a moment. Then she took an opaque jar from the cupboard. She scooped up a little cream from it and smoothed it over her hands. She raised her palms to her nose and inhaled the perfume. Her face was a picture of anticipation.

I stopped breathing for a moment. And there was a great stillness in the room before she laughed and, taking up her jacket and things, said, Let us go then. You and I have a bus to catch.

I swept up my books quickly and started to follow her to the door. I turned back and, with wild care, propped the letter against the blue glass jug on the table.

The trees were scrabbling at the edges of the wide, green paddock. The air was glacial, the light fracturing. Clouds were massaging the sky and their shadows fell like a dark pendulum over the land as the wind made water and waves of the tussocks in the blue light. We rode past a herd of Aberdeen Angus, their Scottish faces turned towards us in alarm at our approach.

An iron gale arose and tore in from Bass Strait. The distant sound of a bell ringing was chopped in and out by the wind. Clouds formed in waves and broke in the sky. The horses were skittish, tugging on the reins, picking a path through fallen wood. Queenie pranced sideways around a stump, shying at a wombat that stumbled into our path, miserable with the mange eating away at it, making it blind.

Soon we reached the dense forest of tall, straight swamp gums, blackwood, twisted ti-tree, musk, blanketwood, hazel and currant bush. It was the part of our place closest to Cape Liptrap. To the east lay the Bald Hills and Waratah Bay and the wrecks of *Alcandre* and *Rubicon*. We were within two miles of the sands where whales' skeletons floated in the sea. A bloodwood seeped red resin. Toadstools were acidic orange on a deep blue branch. A bird's song of alarm cut up the thickening air.

I slipped off the Appaloosa and he snorted, leaning his breast into me, steaming his warm smell into the air. There was the rich scent of sods, the pungent odour of organic decay. The temperature was dropping more quickly than anticipated. I could imagine where the mercury would be on the gauge nailed to the verandah post at the back door, where I had seen my father tapping the falling glass the night before, fearing the full development of an intense low.

The clouds were swollen shapes, dark masses, groaning with their load. Rain was coming in from the slapping sea. It would be a deluge.

Ariane climbed off Queenie behind me and let her feed. She held the reins loosely and ran her hand along the silk of her neck, her face smudged with flung hair. I think…, she started anxiously. The creamy flesh tones of her face had bleached to a pallid ash; she was dematerialising in the frayed light.

I think we should head back now, Madeleine. I admire your intrepid adventures but really, the weather is changing…

The rain was like a dark filter over the day.

My father will be here soon, I replied. He said we should wait for him so he can see the bones, too. He hasn't seen them yet.

She stepped on a twig, which sharply snapped, and she looked behind her.

Tying up the horses quickly, I beckoned to her and led her to the darkest place in the wilderness, where the vines dragged down from the trees and the black peat was always moist. Exposed tree roots lay like snakes in the grass. I indicated the grave in the small clearing in the skewed trees where I had left the spade. She bent her head to protect herself from the rain and a strand of hair wisped at the edge of her mouth. When she looked back at me, her eyes were white in a face turned dark by fear. She drew her hair from her face with a gesture that spoke of a weary sort of submission. There was only the sound of a crake's breaking voice, the soft grunting of the horses.

A flash of lightning entombed the scene.

⌒

The gathering cattle stood with their gleaming black backs to the white rain, seeking shelter under trees. The horses' hooves, hurrying towards home, slipped on the grass, bright with the sluicing rain. I gripped Queenie's reins more firmly and brought her closer to the Appaloosa. Trees were bent so low that they were dragging in the rising water. The wind ripped at my soaking hair and my lips cracked. A tree nearby split, shrieking in a flash of light, and the horses, shocked by the violent birth of the storm, swerved sideways through pools of water dimpled by rain.

By the time I had made my way along the bleak stretch back to the house and let the horses go in their paddock, I was drenched and covered in the heavy smell of earth. My father's strawberry clover was drowning in the water creeping over the land up to the house, making the roads impassable.

In the shed on the other side of the house, I lifted the saddles onto the wooden beam where they were kept. I could see that the car had not yet returned. The rain was drilling into the earth all around me. The icy wind swept off the rising white floodwaters and struck my wet clothes, making my skin turn blue.

Minutes later my mother and Isabelle appeared suddenly through the olive tones of the drenching rain. My mother called into the face of the gale as they hurried towards me, through the swells of ti-tree, across earth stuck in its own glug, sludge, each picking up armfuls of wood. Everything was strewn, broken. There was a wreckage of branches, bark stripped from trees, skins of plants, broken webs, and thistle stalks like wild duck feathers flying upwards in the gale.

Come inside, Madeleine! cried my mother, but the rain soaked her words before they reached me.

Isabelle hurried ahead through bursts of static to open the screen door and we stacked the wood in the woodbox beside the Aga to dry as the wind rose again and a chair outside crashed down onto the verandah with a sound that made my heart leap. Simultaneously came the thunder, and brilliant, jagged bolts of lightning illuminated the room.

It was a long time before we heard the sound of oilskins brushing at the door, and saw my father come in, the water dripping from his hat. There was an urgency in the way he reached for the black telephone to ring a neighbour to get the latest reports about the flood. We heard him yelling down the line as rain drummed on the corrugated iron roof, so loud that I couldn't hear my own thoughts. He told us that a ship had foundered in the heavy surf, and I remembered hearing the bell's voice breaking and rolling in on the wind. Someone had been pulling the bell-rope down on the beach.

The rain fell down the chimney, the power failed and the oil lamps were lit as cold crept through the house. A door banged open. I moved to the hearth to warm myself, and stared at the intensity of the flame.

That night, with the rain beating at the roof, it was like sleeping tied to the tracks in the path of an approaching train.

On the night after the deluge, I saw the moon wading towards me through the lavish darkness, grappling with the black trees, thrusting them aside until it was full in the sky for a moment. The shadows were crosshatched about me as I sat bleary-eyed in bed. All through the watery night, on successive waves of sleep I heard the name *Ariane*.

The next days and nights passed dimly, with the memory of water like a blanket across my brain. I slept for days, wearing my father's socks and curled up, bound in the safety of sleep, cocooned. I was waking and dreaming—part of each world, belonging to neither. I lifted my head and heard a charcoal nocturne playing somewhere, a river of music flooding down the passage into my room, the final note prolonged on the air and hardly ending. Then I was falling again, diving down to the bottom of the sea of sleep and settling on the sand there, dreaming of that which was irrecoverably lost. It was dark, the moon obscured, and the shape of my fate frightened me. There were lights far off, moving in the trees like lanterns searching against the black sky. A crake swung by my window with a cry like the last sound a human makes.

My mother wiped my forehead with a cool flannel and I roused. In my dream there had been something curled about my back in the bed: a long skin left by a snake in the night.

I listened for my mother's step upon the wooden floor. I slept and woke again to find she was still with me. There was a break in the sky; the moon had sloughed off the dark skin of cloud. The sour rain had stalled and in the morning the water had receded. Beyond the window the land was covered in a shawl of spider webs as far as I could see, making their own silver sea. The light waved like a breeze, and the whole room was lit. There was a whistling in my lungs when I breathed, as though a bird were caught there. Isabelle brought me tea and sat with me as I began coughing up pearls of phlegm. She read aloud to me deep into the night.

After a week the doctor came, suspecting the sleeping sickness caused by hydatids worming in my brain, lulling it into a torpor. He said that it would take time for me to recover.

My father drove me to the convent to collect some schoolwork, for the doctor had advised that I stay away from school until completely well. He thought some French books would help me recuperate and amuse me during my convalescence. I looked out of the window on the journey there and did not speak, for I had woken from my sleep a stranger to myself.

Sister Paulinus stood in front of us, her large hands uncomfortably crossed before her. Her wide mouth was pressed into a straight line, her eyes creased and dark. A frown on her face. The cross hung against the black curtain of her habit. Her companion, Sister Maria, silently watched her while she told my father that during the flood Ariane had left the school suddenly, without a word to anyone. That they were all so disappointed and, she hinted, not a little hurt by her sudden, unexpected departure.

There had been a mysterious letter, apparently. Mrs Teasdale had found it when she noticed Ariane's absence.

On the way home we stopped at the yellow house and my father and I sat at Mrs Teasdale's kitchen table as she retold the story. Most people thought that Ariane had left everything after the chaos caused by the flood, gone back to Paris, but Mrs Teasdale had her doubts, she told my father. The police came, searched the drawers, cupboards and closets in her room and took away some of her things, including some clothes. The police thought that the letter explained the situation.

I never read such a thing, said Mrs Teasdale, pursing her lips. She drew a copy of the letter from her apron pocket and handed it to my father to read, then moved to straighten a tablecloth, her turned back assembling itself into a rebuke. I noticed that the pages were curled in the manner of a document that had been re-read many times.

With quiet deliberation, my father took the letter, stood up and walked to the window, looking out. He removed his glasses and pressed his forefinger to his forehead, pushing up the skin.

He reset his glasses upon his nose and read the letter.

On my father's face, an expression I recognised but could not name. He forgot himself a moment, and went to put the letter in his pocket as if it belonged to him.

❧

I went for a ride alone, with Feather trotting close to my side. Suddenly, near the river, I came across my father kneeling, his back hunched, his leg flung awkwardly to one side, a hand to his forehead as I'd seen him in mass. His gumboots were trimmed in black peat; his hair hung down across his face. His ankle, which had once been broken in a fall from his horse, would be aching in the cold. The gloom lowered; the pockets of grass shone a wet green. He moved his head towards me when he realised I was there. He turned abruptly away, stood up, walked to his horse and rode off.

Then there was my wild gallop across the paddock. I rode bareback, flung out along the horse's body like hair.

That night my father told me that soon we would be leaving Tarwin.

Isabelle was crying in her room, not wanting to leave.

❧

Our car had owlish headlights, a chrome bumper bar and a grille across the front. I placed my hand on the curve of the bonnet, then pulled the silver door handle out towards me and got in beside Isabelle, behind my mother. My father handed me a small suitcase and climbed in to the driver's seat. And there was just my mother's hand in a white glove, reaching out from a stretch of dark clothing to close the door, and the car in the settling dusk on the pale road.

A wet leaf on the windscreen was like a piece of stained glass in the last ray of light. My father pointed the front of the car towards the bridge and slowly we rode over the moving wooden boards. On the other side, water crept at the wheels. We left behind a sheet thrown over a pile of stacked furniture, exposed lightbulbs, and a fallen picture. My father's face flashed in the rear-vision mirror.

⌒

I became even more alert to the danger of beauty in women after that. I studied the power of beauty and the way that we are delicately held in its thrall. I slept with my window open to the moon when it was full, because I had read that the moon could make you beautiful. Every month for years, I bathed in the moon's blue light.

I avoided beauty in others. Carefully, quietly, I avoided it because it made my heart bleed. It was as though beauty bruised me, injured me: beauty was the fin cutting across the sea towards me.

Night swimming

I slip out the back entrance of the lycée and catch the train back into the centre of Paris. Walking up the rue de Rivoli towards my apartment, I turn left and enter the hair salon in the rue des Mauvais Garçons, sealed from the noises of the street by thick glass.

A young man clothes me in a white linen robe and ties it at my waist. He places a ticket in the cuff and I make my way up the circular staircase to the washing room. My hair is loosened now and unwinds upon my shoulders, a veil across my face for a moment before he takes my head, bracketing a hand beneath my chin, one at my forehead, and bends it back. I surrender to the warmth of water as my hair is gathered and washed. Lulled by the hypnotic motion of the hand upon the head, the massaging of the scalp, the warmth of the water, the honey silkiness of the shampoo, I dream of ancient Rome, when the ornatrix was specially trained in the art of hair arranging. Floral tapestries were woven from the hair of a hundred members of the same family.

When it is time to rise, I reluctantly descend the staircase. Gently propelled, I am seated near the window. In the mirror I see the woman beside me emerging from the flashing scissors.

It's different. It's different, she cries sharply.

Armand bends my head forward.

This swimming, Madeleine, it destroys your hair.

He is surprised when I ask him to cut it all off.

As he concentrates on his task, I glance up for a moment. My face is white in the mirror and my long, black hair slips and winds about my neck as he cuts. He gently bends my head forward again and, closing my eyes, I feel my hair being shed down over my shoulders. A heavy weight let loose, it tumbles onto the shining wooden floor as Armand snips rapidly, carving my remaining hair to make a beautiful shape.

Someone has taken the seat beside me. A small dog curls up next to her expensive Italian shoes. She speaks to Armand in a deep, honey voice and inquires about his health as a second hairdresser approaches.

What would you like done today, Madam?

Nothing out of the ordinary, the magnificent voice replies. Simply make me beautiful, as usual.

As Armand lifts my head, I see in the mirror a square-faced woman of great ugliness. She catches my eye and laughs at my surprise.

⌒

Night swimming is a ritual I first took up after going with Xavier to see the Musée de l'Orangerie and the treasure it contained, the swimming waterlilies. For this last time I walk along the Seine. On the Ile St-Louis I step into a small shop and buy a package of *za'atar* as a last gift for Xavier. As I cross the bridges to the rue de Pontoise and the swimming pool, I can smell the spicy mixture of ground sumac berries, toasted sesame seeds and dried thyme.

The blue of the pool reminds me of the thirteen-year-old girl who, in 1876, slipped on the ice and fell into a deep coma. When she awoke, thirty-two years later, she said that her only memories of the lost decades were of great darkness and blue men. She had been captured, stilled in blue.

There are few people present at the pool this evening. I examine them closely. Some lie, laced on the diving boards, pulling down the legs of their bathers. There are only one or two swimmers gleaming in the water. I take a white towel and walk to the edge of the illuminated pool.

My skin is losing its whiteness, and becoming crinkled around the toes from the swimming I do each night. The pool stretches out before me and I fold myself into the water, which clothes me in silk: it is warmer than the air but not as warm as my blood, so I quickly pull the goggles down over my eyes and slip under. My new hair feels light. Immediately my thoughts dissolve in the water.

Deep in the pool I can see ahead of me the blue water and the lights dazzling at the bottom. The water moves against my skin and I reach my arms into it, hardly disturbing the surface at all. My hands break it gently and quietly, and my arms dip in and out, pulling me along silently with a lazy ease to the cadence of my strokes. Gaining speed, I lean down upon my shoulders and my arms rotate through the water before me, conducting my passage. I take longer, deeper strokes, pausing upon the wave against the side of my face, slumbering lazily upon it for a moment before waking into the next stroke, then swelling forward again. Already I am halfway up the pool and moving faster, sweeping through the water, displacing it so that my body can pass easily through. Small bubbles press themselves between my fingers and rise in circles of light. At the end I do a tumble turn and feel the water streaming through my hair, waving at my body as I stretch forward, my legs driving me on again. Breathing heavily, my arms are spinning through the water now, blood filling my heart.

When I have swum enough, I pause and draw air down into my lungs. I climb out of the pool at the deepest end and lean over the water. It looks as deep as a volcanic lake, and the eyes there meet mine. I am suspended for the fall. My body curves as I dive deep and swim along the blue tiles at the bottom with my head, my breasts and shoulders arched back, my legs above me. When I meet the air, it is as though I slip out of my skin, out of my body, and become some wild sea creature in a dream, scooping bubbles of light, my breath stilled for a few moments before I dive down again.

Then I surface quietly, like a peaceful thought.

Xavier opens the door. He stands there looking at my freshly cut, damp hair. He touches it with the back of his hand. My face follows the motion of his hand. His forefinger traces my newly revealed neck, the swollen skin around my eyes where my swimming goggles have been.

Oh good. I can get high on chlorine tonight.

We walk out into the street with its smell of roasting chestnuts. The moon is a black cat's eye, half closed in the night. For many years Xavier has frequented a jazz club on the rue des Halles. He usually sits at a table with the same group of friends. There is a loyalty about them, and the way they greet new musicians.

This evening he leads me through the press of people, down the wooden staircase, and we sit at the end of the long table. I am allowing myself to be led because the swimming has made me drowsy. As I turn to watch, I can feel him move a little closer to me. He taps his fingers on my arm, places his hand upon my wrist and listens with me. The music is loud, hot and fast. Added to it are the sounds of chairs scraping back quickly, the clattering of plates and glasses, the smell of sweat and espresso coffee, the haloes of grey cigarette smoke.

Then there is a change in tempo and the crowd settles. Music blossoms from the sax. As though we are floating on the surface of the music, Xavier draws me to my feet and we begin to dance. We have not done this before in public. Some time ago he suggested that he teach me how to dance. And we had practised a little in his apartment. But I knew he never danced because the others had told me, laughing. There were women in the group who would have loved to dance with him.

So he takes me into his arms and smiles as I try to get my feet to move the right way. He lifts up my chin so that I cannot see my feet. He makes me look at him. And it is there. Desire. I relax and move with him through the music.

We return to the rue de Médicis with the night opening and closing on the moon. Because Xavier is with me, I feel secure.

I found something precious today, he says, and leads me to the sofa.

Years and years ago I was in Sydney, and I saw this very performance. I was in the audience. Now, today, I found a tape of it. Watch this.

He is beside himself with the excitement of his good fortune. He plays the tape and I see Joan Sutherland singing *Lucia* in the opera house by the listening harbour. The mad scene. The dark web of hair trailing down onto the long, white nightgown, the streaks of blood, the knife still in her hand. In her madness she was unaware of her appearance, indifferent to its meaning. Such is Xavier's absorption in the voice that he does not see the expression on my face.

He wraps his arms around me. It is the scent of him that I drink first. Taking my hand, he leads me to the bedroom and places his other hand upon my throat and slides it up under my jaw. He holds my face and keeps it there, his head thrown back a little. He puts his ear to my heart as though listening for the sound of the sea in a shell. When he speaks of love, he enunciates his words clearly as if he is speaking to a deaf woman, or someone who doesn't know the language.

I am swimming as his hands make a curve of my body, and it arches down again, diving into him. And I lose my weight, lose direction in the swirl of the dive. There is a tangle of hips, thighs, sinewy ribs, breasts and long shinbones. I am swollen and soft as he pushes his face into my body, along my bones, his hands finding their way to the warm, flowing parts of me.

The silence now as we move together like divers on the sea floor. And then, when he murmurs, *Ma belle Madeleine*, as always without irony, there is a sense of great lightness before the amnesia of sleep comes, pressing down upon me like a pillow, sweeping me over the edge of night.

Before dawn I creep out of his arms. During the night his long body has settled around the curve of mine. He has folded his warmth around me, the hollows in his body like depressions, mauve waves in the sand. He does not wake. Rising from the bed in the dark, I pick up my clothes, my boots. I shiver a little. I am slipping my moorings.

In the bathroom, where the night lamp casts some light on the floor, I dress. I drop one boot on its side and he stirs, murmurs my name. Standing quite still, I hear his breath become heavy again, and wait until he has settled back into sleep. Then I draw out the letter from the pocket of my coat and place it on the table. Becoming aware of some movement, I pause a moment, just long enough to see the headlights of a passing car slash across Bluey's eye. The bird is hunched, watching me closely as I quickly slip out into the street, the flood of air.

The street-sweeping machine is making its way along the rue de Médicis. I am hit in the face by the diesel fumes from the truck, and suck them in, sniff them up, for with them comes the perfume of grass, flattened and made a luminous green by a sour rain. Even in the early morning, in the dimness, there are shadows. Turning into the rue de Vaugirard, I am met by water rushing up out of the drains and gushing loudly along the gutter. A black man in a vest washes water over the stone with a great broom—scrubbing, scrubbing the streets.

I walk up the middle of quai St-Bernard, my shoes shouting on the cobblestones. Ahead there is a person or a tree standing in the pale first light. The mist is like a hat pulled down over my eyes. A man walks along with his head moving from side to side, like a soldier alert for ambushing guerrillas in the scrub. He carries, in a transparent plastic bag, a cabbage that looks like a head. The square lamps give an orange light. A shutter moves at a window. The airport bus comes for some tourists and the voices of Australian children echo in the empty street. I am tired. My skin drags on my bones.

There has been a storm in the night and people have left broken umbrellas in bins along the street, flung aside like dead cormorants. I cross the Seine. The lights on the black water, curves of light under the bridges and their distorted reflections, are like Chinese calligraphy. I glean the close smell of imminent rain.

I see a white dog slinking along the street.
Mon cœur, I whisper to it as it passes.

⌒

The train sweeps me away from the Gare de Lyon and Paris, turning me against the pull of gravity. Its hollow, drawn-out singing makes a sound like instruments in an orchestra tuning up for a concerto. This journey, like others, no matter how small or how mundane, no matter what its purpose, causes my pulse to quicken. Every journey I take repeats that other journey when I rode through the icy rain into the darkness, and put beauty in its grave.

The white river of early-morning mist begins to run faster outside the train. The air finally gives way and lets through the rain as the conductor removes his sunglasses and leans towards me for my ticket. He mistakes me for someone who knows where she is going. In *Breathless* Michel tells Patricia that Italy's the place to go. I am heading for the darkest corner of the forest, because that is where I came from. I'm heading for Ravello and Isabelle.

Like the Chinese swallow that regurgitates the crumbly white strips of Japanese moss to build its nest, I am spewing memory. What I have been is collapsing in mid-flight. It must be Isabelle to whom I go. To tell the story in a vast unburdening, because, like me, Isabelle has killed what she loved. The thought of telling Isabelle everything, the whole story, is like glimpsing a far-off puff of approaching steam, feeling a small vibration on a train track in the empty landscape of my unspooling memory.

When I struck Ariane with the spade, she buckled and then lay on her side like a boat on a beach, stones in her mouth. I saw in my hands the way a skull's walls fall in, blunting the blood cells, brushing the membrane with bone; the sudden dulling of hair, floating circles of blood, her spine a broken column. In that cool and odorous place, in that darkness, I made myself alone. It didn't take long for the rest: the spade in the ground made a sound like tearing sobs. The whip bird spoke again and again.

I remember that I looked around, seeking a trace of absolution, if only that left by a stag in the undergrowth, but saw instead three avian heads on the branch above, watching me. I turned away from them to position the rocks, plucking away a curl of brittle, murdered hair, sloughed from her head.

Now the conductor leaves me, moves on to the next passenger. As we pass a treeless cemetery lying between a railway line and a road, a couple sits down opposite me. He examines his fingernails. The woman feels the lipstick on her lips with her tongue. Their eyes are sharply turned away from each other.

The train is speeding towards Italy. I look at my watch. Xavier would be rising now. He is walking to the bathroom. Sleep is heavy about him and he is looking for me. He thinks that perhaps I am in the kitchen making a bowl of coffee. Because he does not have his glasses on, he does not see the letter at first. It sits on the table, set against the sugar bowl, a square, white envelope.

He sees it now and pauses a moment. Perhaps his heart sinks a little because the envelope has his name on the outside in my handwriting. He takes up the letter and, as he walks towards the light at the window, his hands open it. His fingers are trembling as they slide along the flap, as they tear the paper away. He draws out the letter, unfolds it, and puts on his glasses, turning his back to the window so that the light falls upon the pages. He reads:

Dearest

    By the time you read this, I will be gone. I dreamed of snow last night and knew that I must go.

    Let me tell you.

    My soul stood like a tree, bare in winter when I came to this foreign land, my heart askew, like a bird flailing across continents. I did not expect to find my resting-place here with you and kept our love like a secret in a silk sack that I wore between my breasts.

    Like a monk at his manuscript, I have studied you, and the gift that you are. You are the light at a paper window. You have reached the centre of me, opened me like a precious letter. I travelled with you in the night and will not forget the journeys that we took into the deep heart.

    I am with you there always…

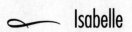 Isabelle

In Ravello, Isabelle sits on a wall at Villa Cimbrone above the Gulf of Salerno, sheltered from the summer wind by orange trees. Amid the violets in the grass, the steps to the Terrazza dell'Infinito are waves upon the sea. The throat of a bird swelling with the dew of evening makes an arch against the sky.

The coast turns pink and she becomes aware of the shadow and its fall, so she leaves the garden and makes her way along the walled lanes to catch the bus down to Amalfi, where she will meet Luca at the Caffè Pompeii. She walks down the via dei Fusco, past the Hotel Villa Amore. They have brought the sidewalks in. A cat growls at her from the top of a stone wall and a light flashes in the evening as a window closes. There are nets strung through the groves to catch the oranges as they fall.

She reaches the piazza, where some men are loading sand into the saddlebags upon two forlorn donkeys. Before she passes into the tunnel that leads to the bus stop, she touches one of the animals upon the neck.

Waiting for the Sita bus in the dusk, Isabelle hides from the wind on the steps of a garden hanging over the Amalfi Coast. A little boy comes and sits beside her on the steps, his schoolbag on his back, his face a lamp. As they wait together, he seems to sense her anxiety to be on her way, and he whispers reassuringly to her in the dark, Sita is coming.

It grows colder there on the edge of the high garden. She hears other whispers in the dark. The boy looks up as a black car comes to a sudden stop beside them, seeming to draw itself together like a dog ready to lunge. He jumps up and steps in front of Isabelle as the men approach her.

The boy does not know the language they speak. It is the cut-glass sound of Katoomba cold he hears in their voices as one puts out an arm to shepherd Isabelle into the waiting car. And with a muffled screech of tyres, the car swings around the piazza and takes Isabelle back through the tunnel. It winds her down to Amalfi, away from the boy. Falling away from Ravello.

⌐

She hears the scratching sound of a cigarette lighter. In one fluid movement the detective in the passenger seat raises his hand to the ceiling of the car. He turns on the light. His hand is as white as a glove. He spreads a map on his knees, seeking the way back to Naples, and so on.

And he speaks to her while his silent companion drives on into the night along the treacherous road. Where's your sister?

My sister? Madeleine had nothing to do with it, she replies, confused.

He turns away then, his eyes in shadow.

How did you find me? she asks.

The detective takes out the photograph of her and Madeleine, taken so long ago.

Dr Rose found it and gave it to us.

He reads to her from a piece of paper, much smaller than the map, a piece of paper with words and official stamps on it. But it is the other story that grips Isabelle—the spaces, the deep gorges of silence between written words. Her hand finds its way to her pocket now and her fingers, rubbing the worn silk as if it were a rosary bead, read the contents of the blue sack: a brooch, a little box, a half-empty packet of cigars, a used Italian train ticket, and a curled and faded black and white photograph of a bell.

Madeleine would come too late.

In the Caffè Pompeii Luca would be waiting, working on the portrait, keeping an ear on the sounds of the evening outside: a dog barking, the car driving too quickly along the road outside the piazza. From the lamp above the door, light falls upon a membrane of ultramarine. He is painting Isabelle in soft mauves, standing in currents of light in his garden. She imagines him dipping his brush in the palest yellow, a film of green earth pigment. There is a purity about his treatment of hues. He uses ancient purple dyes here and there—blatta, oxyblatta, hyacinthina—and pieces of cloth interwoven with minute birds' feathers.

It is growing cooler. He is putting on a jacket and picking up his brush, a long cone of soft bristles. He holds his brush as though it were a pen and she's there in his garden again:

There is a long phrase between the night notes, the end notes by the bell, then this brimming morning reverie in windflowers, Italian lavender, sea anemones and *Bellis perennis*. Slaked lime and marble dust make polished plaster of the air; the budding gardenia rests a heavy head; dogwood leaves lie against the sky like boats on still water. In the weeping mulberry a swaying worm spits silk. An azalea flower drops to the earth, like a bright pink origami bird.

In this generous dwelling, a breath away from summer, she stands in the mosaic of the moment, listening for the next note of the struck bell, beneath the desiccating blossom of the pear tree; the sun first upon her head, then shoulders, in sheets of smoking gold. She stands tall and quite still, an iris gloved in green. Around her, forget-me-nots are rocked by bees and she can hear the panting of birds' wings. The scent of bergamot orange is like a veil across her face.

In a pool of night rain, the water swells with light under its skin, reflecting pale iris with yellow throats, stroke after stroke of ixia stacked on pearwood, the luminous muslin spider web, spent flowers like empty cicada shells.

Isabelle looks back through the rear window as the bell from the Duomo sounds for evening mass. She thinks of the books and photographs in the house in Katoomba, and of that last line of Robert Lowell's: *I bell thee home.*

Acknowledgments

Parts of this novel have been published in various forms, as follows: 'The goodbye café', *Westerly*, vol. 47, 2002, pp. 52–66; 'Falling, falling', *Meanjin*, vol. 58, no. 3, 1999, pp. 78–95; 'Imago', *Westerly*, no. 1, Autumn, 1996, p. 105–111; 'Song to the moon', *Familiar Tides*, anthology of Newcastle Poetry Prize, Hunter Writers Centre, Newcastle, 2004.

The Concerto Inn was submitted as part of a PhD in Communication and Media undertaken at the University of Western Sydney.

For encouragement and editorial advice I am indebted to Fran Bryson, Amanda Curtin, Anna Gibbs, Jennifer Maiden, Cassandra Pybus and Terri-ann White.

Also in the New Writing series

Annabel Smith

New Writing

It is a tree house, she begins, a house with roots that go deeper than the trees themselves can reach. It is a house that breathes, that draws life from the soil in which it is planted, that turns its leaves to catch the rain…

Or it is a boathouse, a house that floats, that rises and falls with the tide. It is sometimes anchored, sometimes unmoored: a house that drifts with the current, raises its sails to catch the wind, rides the heaving waves to shore.

ISBN 1 920694 55 2

Grace dreams of designing a house for her lover, Michael, a place where they can begin their life together. But before she can step into her future with Michael, Grace must journey into the past to confront its crippling legacy of silence and secrets.

This lyrical, engaging novel spans two generations and both hemispheres as Grace navigates her new map of the universe. It is a story about grief and passion, architecture and astronomy, but above all it is a story about finding yourself.

Impressive in scope and beautifully written…Grace the protagonist is a character of considerable depth and subtlety.
Justine Ettler, *The Weekend Australian*

In these days of high hysteria and over-wrought narrative, Smith's ability to create tenderness and feeling without excess is welcome.
Helen Elliott, *The West Australian*

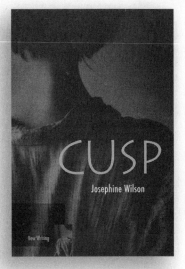

Lena squinted into the searing heat.
How many young women before her
had landed on a February afternoon
and known in their heart of hearts
that they were on the precipice of
delight; that their roaming souls were
soon to be enfolded by the warm glow
of the familiar?

'Not as many as you might think,'
she muttered to herself.

ISBN 1 920694 56 0

On a hot, hard day in 1990, Lena Hawkins reluctantly returns from
New York. In Perth, Mavis Hawkins feels as if she has spent her whole
life waiting. But now her wait is over. Her only daughter is about to
land, and she must tell her the truth.

While Mavis struggles to make her daughter see what is right
before her eyes, Lena's past hounds her, threatening to obscure the
present and the future.

Dark, funny and poignant, *Cusp* explores the profound impact of
time and place on the lives of two women, and questions the things we
value, the places we call home, and the spaces between life and death.

> *...the debut of a wonderful dramatist and storyteller...the idiosyncratic voices
> of the daughter and mother protagonists, Lena and Mavis Hawkins, capture
> attention from the outset and hold it through to the novel's last, moving page.*
> Danielle Wood, *Australian Book Review*

> *Wilson is a master of dialogue that seems to skate along the surface, yet
> conveys an enormous amount.*
> Dorothy Johnston, *The Canberra Times*